A Cowboy's Forever Faithful

SWEET VIEW RANCH
BOOK ONE

JESSIE GUSSMAN

Contents

Acknowledgments

Cover art by Julia Gussman
Editing by Heather Hayden
Narration by Jay Dyess
Author Services by CE Author Assistant

~

Listen to the unabridged audio for FREE performed by Jay Dyess on the Say with Jay channel on YouTube. Get early access to all of Jay's recordings and listen to Jessie's books before they're available to the general public, plus get daily Bible readings by Jay and bonus scenes by becoming a Say with Jay channel member.

Chapter One

"And they lived happily ever after."

Ellen closed the book and brushed her hand over the forehead of her sister, Maeve. She wasn't exactly her sister, since Ellen lived with her Uncle Tadgh and Aunt Ashley, since Uncle Tadgh had raised her after his sister, her mother, had passed away.

Still, she loved Maeve like a sister, and since her aunt and uncle had gone away for three days for a well-deserved anniversary trip, Ellen was in charge of taking care of her and her little brother, Cian.

Cian was already in bed, but Maeve had wanted a story, so Ellen had happily snuggled down with her while the wind roared outside and the promised blizzard moved in, making their little house on the outskirts of Sweet Water, North Dakota, feel cozy and warm.

Ellen wasn't worried about the weather. She might have been born in Ireland, but she'd lived with her uncle in North Dakota for more than a decade. They had left Ireland so long ago she didn't even remember it.

From the doorway of the room, Chewy, her Australian Cattle Dog, whined. Chewy was heavy with pups and due to whelp any day. Ellen was a little concerned since she had never delivered puppies before. But she wasn't anticipating any problems.

"Can I sleep with Chewy?" Maeve said sleepily from her cozy position snuggled underneath the big blankets.

"No. Not tonight. I need to keep her close to me just in case she decides to have those puppies tonight." It would be a good night for Chewy to become a mom with all the wind and snow and the blizzard conditions. A perfect night for a dog to have her puppies.

A little bit of unease went through Ellen. She hadn't been very concerned. Dogs had puppies all the time without any help. But for her to be alone, with her aunt and uncle gone, the storm raging outside, and her unable to leave because she was responsible for her brother and sister, it put a different spin on things.

Plus, even if there was a problem, she wouldn't expect Lark to drive through a storm like this. Everyone who had a lick of sense had stocked up on the essentials and hunkered down to wait it out. North Dakotans were tough, but they weren't stupid.

Ellen was eighteen years old, an adult. Old enough to handle any problems that might come up.

Her little personal pep talk didn't really help.

A harsh wind hit the house so hard the walls shook, and Ellen cast Chewy a worried glance before she bent down, kissing her sister's forehead before tiptoeing out of the room, flipping off the light switch as she went, and closing the door softly behind her.

The house was dark and quiet. Unusually so. Ellen still had four months of her senior year left, but she'd turned eighteen in October and was legally an adult. She didn't feel like it though. She still felt like a kid at heart, even though people told her she was more mature than normal children her age. She certainly had more responsibility than most kids her age. She had her own business raising Highlander cattle and another business training, and now breeding, Australian Cattle Dogs.

She was making as much money as a full-grown man, and still she was a full-time student in high school.

Chewy whined as Ellen went to the living room to look outside at the snow coming down in big gusts. Ellen dropped to one knee and used both hands to take Chewy's head and hold it.

"Is it time?"

She didn't think she was going to be scared, but the idea of Chewy having her puppies in the snowstorm while Ellen was alone and couldn't call for help sent tendrils of fear with icy claws down her backbone.

She had been looking forward to snuggling up on the couch and reading a good book by candlelight while the snow came down, but this new development made that seem less and less appealing. How could she relax when Chewy could be in distress?

Without even really thinking about it, she pulled her phone out of her back pocket and sent a text to her best friend in the whole world. Travis.

> I think Chewy is going to have her babies tonight. I'm scared.

She couldn't admit that to just anyone, but Travis knew everything about her. They texted often. Back when she was younger, around fourteen, she'd had a huge crush on him and had been insanely jealous of the cheerleader who seemed to catch his eye.

But they had come to an agreement, and she had decided to be the very best friend that she could possibly be to him. And he had become her best friend in return. He confided in her about his business and the hardships he went through. She could tell him things that she couldn't tell anyone else, and she could trust him. Just as he could trust her.

Most of their communication had been via letters, although in the last few months, they had begun texting more.

His answer came back almost immediately.

> Is she having trouble?

> I don't think so. I just...don't know what to do if she does. The weather is bad.

They'd talked about the weather earlier. He was in Fargo at a business convention, but he knew that her aunt and uncle were going away and she was responsible for her siblings. She had been a little bit worried about taking care of the kids during a blizzard, but she wasn't expecting anything to happen and she watched the children often. That was nothing new.

Delivering puppies? Now *that* was new.

> You've delivered plenty of calves. I don't think puppies are any more difficult than that. But I'll pray for you.

She smiled at his words. Of course. She didn't have to worry. God was in control. Still, with all the responsibility on her shoulders, she wouldn't be human if she didn't feel concern. Plus, she didn't want anything to happen to Chewy.

She said a couple of prayers of her own. And then sent a text back.

> Thank you. You just reminded me of where my priority is supposed to be and who I'm supposed to trust.

He had been really good for her in that regard. Always pointing her to Jesus. Like a good friend should.

He wasn't that far away since he was attending a conference in Fargo with Ford Hansen.

She had been excited because she thought she was going to get to see him. With the blizzard, she didn't know if their travel plans would change, but she had been expecting to see him come back to Sweet Water, visit his family some, and her, and...she thought maybe he was coming home to stay.

He had said four years ago that he was going to be gone for four years, then he was coming back. It had been four years.

She smiled. Because she was graduating soon. She had all kinds of plans for her future, plans that included her Highland cattle and Australian Cattle Dogs. Starting with Chewy's first litter.

Chewy shoved a cold, wet nose into Ellen's hand and whined again.

"Let's go to your bed," she said, indicating the bed that she had made up a week ago in the mudroom.

Her aunt and uncle were awesome. She had been planning on Chewy having her babies in the barn, but they had insisted that Ellen make a bed for Chewy in the house where it would be warmer.

It was called the mudroom because that was the room that everyone came in when they had been outside. They kept their boots, coats, and hats there and washed their hands at the sink. It was just as clean as the rest of the house but had a tendency to get dirty in the spring and fall when things were more wet than usual. It was a nice, cozy place for Chewy, and one where she would feel comfortable, Ellen was sure.

Shoving her phone back in her pocket, she got a glass of water from the tap and walked out to the mudroom.

Sitting down at the edge of Chewy's bed, she patted beside her, and Chewy walked onto the cushions, sniffing and whining and nosing around.

She lay down, then sniffed her side as though trying to figure out what was going on in there.

She whined again.

Several hours later, Chewy had been up and down at least twenty times. Ellen had been unable to concentrate on the book she was reading on her phone, and she had ended up getting up and scrubbing Chewy's water and feed bowls, which were both already completely clean, and beginning to organize the drawer full of gloves and hats and scarves.

With two small children, there were a lot of winter things in the mudroom, and Ellen had everything organized and had leaned against the sink, contemplating scrubbing it down, when her phone buzzed with a text.

She smiled when she saw it was from Travis.

How's Chewy?

Restless.

Chewy was not acting like herself at all. And while Ellen knew that there wasn't anything to be concerned about, not yet, anyway, she still couldn't get herself to settle down.

Is she pushing?

No. She just won't rest. She's up and down and up and down, and she whines and then bites at her side.

It definitely sounds like she's going to have them tonight. How many do you think she's going to have?

He was trying to get her mind off her worries. She smiled at his attempt. That was what a good friend did. Even though he was at a conference and probably should be paying attention to something other than her. Or maybe it was over for the day.

I want her to have at least three. But I'm hoping she has more.

She wanted to keep a few to train and sell them as trained cattle dogs. She had been training other people's dogs. They'd bring them when they were ready, and she would keep them for six or eight months, until they had the commands down and were ready to go back to their homes as a dog with a job, rather than just as a pet.

She loved teaching a dog that it could be a help, and loved even more seeing the dog fall in love with its job, doing what it was bred and born to do. They were so happy when they figured out that they could do what they were driven to do, and they could be rewarded for it.

Most dogs were eager to work, and while training was never easy, they were eager to learn.

She couldn't imagine trying to train a dog who didn't want to work. That was one of the things that was so good about Chewy. She hoped she would pass that drive to work down to her puppies.

Are you going to name one after me?

She laughed.

Sure. I can name one Silly if you want me to.

Ouch. Really?

> Really. If you want me to name a puppy
> Travis, just say so.

> I want you to name a puppy Travis.

> All right. I'll pick the prettiest girl and give her
> that name.

> I don't know why people always say you're
> so nice. I'm not experiencing that niceness
> right now.

She laughed and sent a smiley face emoji. He knew she wasn't going to name any girl dogs Travis, but she actually was already planning on naming the first boy pup after him. After all, Travis had supported her for as long as she could remember. They'd been good friends, and he'd always been around to help her when she needed it.

Not tonight. She would really love to have him around tonight. She almost sent a text back and asked him about the conference, but she thought he might be busy socializing. That seemed to be a lot of his job, making contacts, gathering information, and using everything he learned in any way he could to help build whatever business he was working on. He and Ford had started several. But Travis had confided to her that he couldn't wait to get back and be a farmer because that was his first love.

She wanted things to work out for him and knew that spending time with Ford was the best way for that to happen, even if it meant that she didn't get to see him.

As she turned from the sink, where she had grabbed a rag and started wiping one of the spigots, she saw that Chewy had laid out on her side, and it looked like she was pushing. Finally.

Suddenly she let out a whine, or more like a yell, and Ellen dropped to her knees beside her dog who barely noticed she was there.

Suddenly she was more scared than she'd ever been in her life before. So she did the only thing she knew to do. She started to pray.

She was only on her knees for a couple of minutes before the back door opened and icy wind blew in. She lifted her head and jumped up, thinking that she hadn't shut the door tight, and the wind had blown it open, but there in the doorway stood her best friend, Travis.

Chapter Two

Travis stood in the doorway and stomped the snow off his boots, then grabbed his hat and took it off before stepping in and closing the door behind him.

"Travis?" Ellen said, sounding shocked. He didn't think she would be surprised. Didn't she know that if she needed him and it were possible at all for him to come, he would?

"That's right, short stuff. I'm here." He tried to act like it was perfectly normal for him to drive several hours in a snowstorm to get to her. "I guess this is the mom-to-be," he said, seeing Chewy lying on her bed. It was very unusual that the dog hadn't even gotten up to welcome him. He'd never seen her lie flat out when anything was going on. Chewy was always involved in the middle of everything, a happy, energetic, obedient dog who was completely loyal to Ellen.

Travis loved the dog, just because Ellen did.

"I'm so glad you're here," Ellen said, nodding a yes to his question.

"Well, I don't know what I'm going to do. I don't know anything about delivering puppies."

"You can hold my hand and remind me that I don't need to be afraid."

"Okay. I can do that."

He tried to give a reassuring grin. It was a little disconcerting that Chewy wasn't up greeting him, but he supposed if she was in labor, about ready to have puppies, it was understandable.

"I think she's pushing." Ellen had her eyes glued back on her dog. Her legs stuck straight out, and her side, which had been heaving with each breath she took, was still as her nose pushed out, and her tail lifted.

"Looks like that to me too. It probably takes a bit of pushing before the puppy appears."

"How long do you think?"

"Let's see if we can look it up on the Internet."

"You can take your coat off first. I'm sorry. And I can get you something to drink. Are you hungry?" Ellen seemed to remember that it was polite to offer all those things, and she did them in a rush.

"Let's take care of Chewy first. Although, maybe I'll wash my hands, just because that seems like a good idea." He thought if Chewy needed help, they should have clean hands, but he didn't want to add to Ellen's anxiety by suggesting that something might go wrong.

After he had washed and dried his hands, he knelt down beside Ellen, his eyes on Chewy before he grabbed his phone and searched what to do for a dog in labor.

He read through several articles, since in his experience information on the Internet was not always extremely accurate, and it made sense to see what the general consensus was.

"I think maybe we just need to let nature take its course." He rattled off a few things that they were to look for if Chewy was in distress, but she wasn't displaying any of the signs, other than pushing with no sign of a puppy emerging from the birth canal.

"We should give her more time then?" Ellen asked, the wrinkle in her brows showing her worry and concern.

"Yeah. I think so."

He said that, but he wasn't entirely sure. It seemed like they should be seeing a puppy soon. And if not... He picked his phone back up and read through a few of the things that they said to do if the dog was in distress and the puppy didn't appear.

Another fifteen minutes ticked by, as Ellen stroked Chewy's side and held her breath every time she pushed.

"Here. Hold this." He handed her his phone. Ellen had more experience with delivering animal babies than he did, but sometimes when a person was attached to something and emotionally involved, they didn't perform as well. He thought Ellen could have a cool head no matter what, but he also thought that since he was her friend, he should do it for her.

The next time Chewy tried to push, he moved her tail aside and slipped two fingers into the birth canal.

All he could feel was something solid and slippery, and he assumed it was the puppy, still in the birth sac.

He thought that was a good thing, that the sac hadn't ruptured, but from the way it felt, he thought that perhaps the puppy was sideways in the birth canal or maybe just had its head twisted.

"Does it feel okay?" Ellen asked as Chewy quit pushing and lay there panting.

It was hard to follow her body as it heaved up and down with each breath. But he tried to keep his fingers steady as they felt around, and he tried to make sure that what he thought he felt was actually what he felt.

"Yeah. I think there might be just a little twist, and I'm going to try to move the body so that it's not blocking the birth canal."

"It's stuck?"

He had kind of said that in a roundabout way, but he didn't want to increase the panic he heard in her voice. "I think so. But not badly stuck. Just a little twisted."

"All right," Ellen said softly, and he loved the trust in her voice. Like she believed him when he said it, and also had faith that he could fix it.

Lord, help me to do the right thing.

He had no idea if he was moving it the right way or not; he could be making things worse.

But he was here to help. He had left the business meeting as soon as Ellen had texted him. He'd known she was alone, watching the children tonight, and he'd already been a little worried about her with the blizzard moving in. Most likely, they would lose electricity, and while he knew that Ellen was an old hand at using the woodstove, he hated the thought that she would be there by herself, unable to get in or out and unable to get help if she needed it.

Chewy being in labor was the icing on the cake, and Travis had told Ford what was going on. As he figured, Ford had told him to go right away.

The roads had been fine halfway back to Sweet Water, until he'd hit the edge of the blizzard.

Still, he'd driven in his share of snow, being from North Dakota, and he made it to Ellen with no problem.

Of course, he knew she was going to be fine, but maybe part of the reason that he wanted to go was because he knew that he was leaving the country, probably for several years.

He hadn't told Ellen. He hadn't quite gotten over the disappointment himself. He had thought once Ellen turned eighteen, he could court her the way she deserved and be the boyfriend he wanted to be, rather than the good friend he had been.

Unfortunately, it didn't look like that was going to happen for him for several years.

It had been a long time since he talked to Ellen about his feelings. They'd agreed to be friends, and he'd been the best friend he could be.

He'd also been faithful to Ellen.

This new assignment didn't change anything for him, not in that regard, but he couldn't expect her to sit around and wait for him forever.

Still, Ford Hansen had been good to him; he couldn't tell the man no, especially when Ford was doing everything he could to see that Travis got the best start in life that Ford could give him, learning everything Ford could teach and getting experiences that most men could only dream about.

As he put gentle pressure on the puppy in the birth canal, the sac broke, and water spilled out.

"Her water broke," Ellen said hushed and fast.

"It did." That put more pressure on his shoulders. He needed to get the puppy out without delay. He didn't want it to die in the birth canal.

He felt it wiggle, and he breathed out a silent prayer of thanks. It was still alive.

The broken sac actually made his work a little easier, because he could feel the big head, the tiny paws, and the long body. As he had thought, the head was twisted, and now that the sac had ruptured, he was able to gently pull it around.

He appreciated that Ellen wasn't peppering him with questions. She was beside him, ready to help him if he needed it but also giving him the space he needed in order to concentrate. She'd always been the perfect person to work with.

Chewy pushed, and the birth canal tightened. The puppy wasn't quite in position, and as soon as the pressure eased off, he tugged just a bit more, and the head slid into place. He could tell because the body moved out easily as he pulled his fingers out, like the pup was following him already.

He smiled a little at the thought but didn't allow it to distract him, since he was focused on making sure the little guy had the fluids cleaned out around his nose and watching for that first big breath.

Ellen put her hand on his forearm as she leaned closer, so intent on watching the pup that she probably didn't even realize she was touching him and leaning over top of him.

"I can't see," he teased her.

"Oh. Sorry." She moved back a little, checking to make sure he had a line of sight to the puppy, and then she turned her attention back to it.

In that amount of time, the puppy had taken a deep breath, its little body trembling, as Chewy looked around and started to lick it.

It lifted its head, wobbly and unsure, as Chewy maneuvered just a little so she could continue to clean it off.

"Oh my goodness. It's so adorable," Ellen said, and then she looked up at him with shining eyes. "Thank you. Thank you so much."

"You could have done it."

She nodded, knowing that he was probably right. "But I didn't think to look on the Internet. I didn't think to try to think about what could be wrong. I just…"

"When you get emotionally attached to things, sometimes it's hard to take a step back and look at the situation in an analytical way."

"You mean you're not attached to Chewy?" she asked with her brows raised.

"I am. I love her because you do."

She grinned, knowing that what he said was true. There were probably things that she loved because he did. His brothers for example.

Roger especially had struggled staying on the right side of the law and not going down the path that their parents had gone down. But it didn't matter when he showed up, Ellen always welcomed him into her life and took care of him as best she could. Travis knew she did it because Roger was his brother.

Of course, that was the kind of person Ellen was too. Too nice for her own good sometimes. Although, there really wasn't such a thing. The Bible didn't issue any warnings to Christians about being too nice. It did, however, give lots of exhortations about how Christians needed to be kind.

"Oh! She's pushing again!"

Ellen's words brought his mind back to the fact that while they were out of the woods with the first puppy and it seemed to be doing well, there were more puppies to go.

"Well, she's going to have at least two."

Ellen laughed. "I don't even care how many she has. As long as they're all healthy. I don't want to have to...bury a puppy tonight."

"If you have to, we'll do it together."

He put a hand over her hand that rested on his leg. She looked at their hands for a moment, then looked up into his eyes, her own shining with gratitude and appreciation.

It wasn't exactly the way he wanted her to look at him, but he knew with the news that he had to deliver, it was the best way. It made his heart sad, but he steeled himself.

He knew he was taking a gamble by going out of the country for years. Especially now that she was eighteen and could possibly settle down anytime she wanted to. Although the world would say she was too young, in ages past, people had got married at twelve and thirteen and had been just fine. Modern society encouraged selfishness and self-fulfillment, rather than the biblical mandates of first and foremost being about others and, in particular, a person's family.

Not popular opinions, and ones he didn't go around talking about.

Still, he'd have to put the idea of Ellen being anything more than just a good friend to him away for now. He would be faithful, and hopefully, she would be too. But if she wasn't, he had to trust the Lord, the same way he encouraged her today to trust God for Chewy's benefit.

Another little nose appeared as the first baby wiggled and wobbled its way to Chewy's side. Soon another chubby little body had slipped into the world, and Chewy leaned around to lick it off too.

Each puppy that was successfully born caused Ellen's smile to grow bigger. He enjoyed watching her, just sitting back and seeing her excitement and appreciation and the love she had for her dog.

Because of the work he did and the fact that he was never in one place for very long, he had no pets. It was nice to come and see Ellen with hers. Truly he thought the four years he'd spent in business was enough, but Ford was determined to teach him everything he knew. And as much as Travis would like to just come home and be a farmer, he knew Ford knew what was best for him. Ford had been right about everything so far, and Travis couldn't turn him down.

In the next two hours, Chewy had eight more little puppies, for a total of ten. They all looked like they were going to be different colors, although there was one female, smaller than the rest, who looked like she was going to be marked exactly like her mom.

"That's your favorite, isn't it?" Travis said as Ellen stroked the little body.

"She looks just like Chewy. I can't help thinking that this is how Chewy started life, and that's probably exactly how she looked."

"I have to agree with that. Although, it's after midnight, and Chewy has to be tired. I am."

"And I never fed you," Ellen said, putting her hands on her knees and looking at Chewy nestled up with her puppies before she stood.

"I wasn't here to get fed," Travis said, but his protest was half hearted. Every time he came, Ellen fed him. And she was a pretty good cook, although she had fed him a few things that he would prefer not to eat again. Although he would, just for Ellen.

"I hear you. Come on. Wash your hands, and I'll warm up some supper."

"Tell me what supper was first," he teased, knowing that he would eat no matter what she made.

"Country-fried steak." She laughed a little. "It seems like every time I make this, you show up. I should make it more often."

He chuckled. "It's what I ate the last time I was here. You know how to summon me apparently."

"Apparently. I think maybe I'll try making it every day and see what happens."

Chapter Three

Travis shut the water off after washing his hands and grabbed the towel to dry them with.

"About that," he said, figuring that this was a good opening, although maybe not the best time. He didn't want to upset her while he still had an hour or so he could stay. Her aunt and uncle would not mind him staying if he couldn't get out, but there was no reason for him not to leave. And he didn't want Ellen to get in trouble. Not that they wouldn't totally understand and welcome him into their home if they were there. It was just the idea that he showed up and stayed the night the one time they left.

"About that? What do you mean?" Ellen said, standing at the door to the mudroom with her hand on the knob as he hung the towel back up.

"Let's go to the kitchen," he said, figuring that Chewy deserved a little rest.

He flipped the light off as he left, closing the door behind him and following Ellen to the kitchen where she grabbed a container out of the refrigerator.

"It's not quite as good warmed up, but it will be food and that's better than nothing."

"You make the best country-fried steak I've ever eaten," he said. "I'll eat it warmed up any day."

The smile that turned the corners of her mouth up was pleased and happy, and made him feel good to have put it there. Especially since it was probably going to disappear once he told her his news.

"We're in the kitchen," she reminded him as she dished some steak out on a plate and put mashed potatoes beside it before she put the plate in the microwave. Then she turned with her hands on her hips and eyed him with a serious look. "I'm listening."

"Good. Lots of times, I feel like I'm talking to you and your head's in the clouds somewhere."

"I always listen to you. You know that."

He grinned but didn't admit that she was right, although she was.

Instead, he said, "Ford wants me to go to Brazil. He has business down there, and it's not doing so great. He'd like to see it get turned around, and he said that this would be my best opportunity to get experience."

"Brazil?"

He nodded.

"Do you speak Portuguese?" She tilted her head. "Is that what they speak there?"

"Yeah, although there are some tribal languages too, I believe. Regardless, I don't speak it, although Ford has sent me several links for software and I've started learning. I know how to ask for a beer."

"Well, that's helpful," she said with more than a little sarcasm in her voice.

"Hey. You never know. I suppose if I get captured by headhunters, it would get their attention anyway."

"Headhunters?"

He kicked himself. He shouldn't have joked about that. She probably didn't realize just how much jungle was left in Brazil. He certainly hadn't until he started looking into it. He figured he would be pretty safe where he was going, but it definitely wasn't North Dakota.

"There is still some jungle, but nowhere near where I'm going. I was joking." He lifted his brows and held his hands up to try to get her to believe him as the microwave beeped.

She pressed her lips together, not buying into his protestations of innocence.

"Look, I wasn't trying to get you to worry about me. Ford wouldn't be sending me down if I wasn't going to be safe. You know that."

"I know," she said, but she didn't sound happy.

"And this might surprise you, but God takes care of people in Brazil just as much as He takes care of people in the United States."

"Wow. I could get offended over that statement, because I know it, except I deserved it. Because you're right. I wasn't thinking about God taking care of you at all. I was getting upset because you were going somewhere dangerous, and I thought... I thought you were coming home to stay." She kept her head down as she used a spoon to stir the mashed potatoes and then lifted the plate and put it back in the microwave. She kept her back to him after she pushed start, as though she didn't even want to look at him, which hurt his feelings just a little. Surely she wasn't that mad at him.

"I wanted to. I still do. I... I could tell Ford no." But he didn't want to.

He saw her shoulders go up as she pulled in a deep breath, and then she blew it out slowly. Finally, she turned around until she faced him on the other side of the counter as she pulled one of her lips back and then looked at him.

"Ford has done so much for you, I'm sure you have zero desire to actually do that. Plus, he's been right about everything he's tried to teach you. You... I'm sure you want to do whatever he wants you to."

"Would you give me advice? As a friend?" he asked softly.

"Advice?" She lifted her brows and looked at him.

"You're my friend. You want the best thing for me. What would you say I should do?"

"I say you should do what you think God wants you to do."

"That's the right answer," he said, his eyes narrowing some. And she smiled with a guilty look on her face. She knew she was just parroting what she was supposed to say.

"What do you think I should do?"

"Do you know for sure that God wants you to go to Brazil?" she asked, and he did not miss the note of hope in her voice.

"No. I don't. I feel like it's the right thing to do because Ford has been so good to me. Every single thing that he's asked me to do has been beneficial in ways I hadn't even imagined. I can't imagine that this would be any different. Even though, I really, really do not want to go. Not at all. Not even a little."

"How soon?" She looked at her hands.

"He just told me tonight that he wants me there next week."

"Next week?" she asked, her voice squeaking a bit. "You're going to miss everything in my senior year. You promised to take me to prom!" Then she closed her mouth. Snapped it shut actually, and contrition stole across her face. "I'm sorry. I'm sorry. I'm making this harder for you, and it's already a hard decision. You... I think you should go. You're right. Ford has gone out of his way to make sure that you're equipped to run whatever business you decide to run. And... The last time we talked, you said you'd made more money already than you ever thought you would in your lifetime."

"I'll be able to buy my own farm, and almost certainly pay cash for it, if I do this."

"And that's what you want," Ellen said, and she didn't sound quite as sad anymore. The microwave beeped, but she didn't move to get his food out. "How long?" she asked, and he thought that the smile she pasted on her face was one of those smiles that said "I'm trying to pretend to be happy even though I'm really not."

In a way, that made him happy. He didn't want her to be joyful that he was leaving. Mostly because of her, he wanted to stay. And he never wanted to see her unhappy. Not for anything, but especially not over stuff that he had done. He did truly feel like this was the best decision, and he had no reason to believe that it wasn't what God wanted him to do. Sometimes it could be a little nebulous, trying to figure out the difference between what he wanted and what God wanted.

What he wanted often overshadowed what God wanted, but God did give him people to confide in, to consult, and to give him their advice.

Ford was one of those people, but Ellen was too. She had always been wise beyond her years. Mature and capable. He trusted her and valued her friendship.

"At least two years. But it could be longer. I probably won't be back much, if at all."

"I imagine the plane ride down there is...a really long one."

"Yeah. And the work that is there for me to do is pretty hard and involved. I'll be...busy." Not too busy to talk to his friend, but definitely busy. Especially if he was able to do what Ford was hoping he would and turn the business around, making it profitable.

You could ask her to marry you and take her down with you.

She turned to get the food at the microwave, and Travis closed his eyes against the temptation that thought elicited. He wanted to. He didn't know exactly how she felt about him, but when he was facing the idea of being thousands of miles away from her, for years, the idea of taking a risk like that made sense, except it wasn't fair to her.

She would miss the rest of her senior year. She wouldn't have a high school diploma. She wouldn't graduate. She'd miss her prom and all the other things that high school seniors expected to do. She'd have to leave Chewy. She'd have to leave her Highland cows and the businesses that she'd grown, and give it all up for him.

Yeah, it was tempting, because he wanted it. But if he loved her, he had to make the decision that was best for her, and so he pressed his mouth closed as she set the plate of steaming country-fried steak in front of him.

"So what are you doing between now and next week?" she asked after he said a short prayer over the food.

"I was going to spend tomorrow here, and then Ford has a few things for me to do, plus I have to get ready to go. I haven't seen my brothers in a couple of months."

"I'm worried about Roger," Ellen said right away as she set a glass of water down in front of him and then grabbed one for herself out of the tap.

"Yeah, me too. Have you heard anything?"

"Not really. He just... He seems to be really tempted by the things that the wrong crowd does. I guess there are people who struggle with those kinds of temptations. I really don't, so it's hard for me to understand why he just doesn't turn his back on those things and start working toward something that's good. But I guess we all have our weaknesses."

"We sure do. And you're right. Roger always seems to have been drawn to wickedness and sin. But I know other people who have weaknesses. Alcohol addictions, food addictions, porn and electronic addictions, cheating addictions, any of those things can destroy marriage, although not all of them would necessarily be qualified as sin."

"Well, there were no cigarettes when the Bible was written, so we could hardly be warned about that," she said with a laugh.

"We don't know. Maybe there was. But I think any kind of addiction is dangerous. The Bible clearly says that we should have control over our flesh. If we allow addictions to control us, or if we can't break free of them, then it's a sin, whether or not the actual action is a sin."

"I agree. But I don't think Roger thinks he's really doing anything wrong. He's just kind of skating down the edge. There are some drugs that have been legalized, and of course alcohol and tobacco are legal as well."

"Of course. But if our body is the temple of the Holy Spirit, we shouldn't be putting anything in it that damages it, and that goes beyond alcohol and drugs and cigarettes. After all, potato chips aren't exactly good for you, and yet we put them in our bodies all the time without thinking about it. That's socially acceptable."

"Good point. I hadn't really thought about that."

"Most people don't. We like to have our little things that we like to look at and point our fingers at, you know, the wicked sins that we'd never do. But there are those things we do to our bodies that are almost just as bad. Soda would be another one. There's nothing good in soda. Are we damaging our body just as much by drinking soda as we are by smoking cigarettes? All that sugar, all those empty calories, all of those things that are bad for our heart and for our insulin levels and our weight, and yet Christians are totally okay with people drinking soda and eating potato chips, it's just the cigarettes that we have a tendency to say are sins."

"You always make me think."

"You make me think as well. Actually, because of you, I've delivered puppies."

She laughed. "I'm so glad you came. Have I thanked you? I guess I was a little bit overwhelmed, but thank you. Thank you so much for dropping everything and running to me when I needed you."

"Of course," he said. He wanted to say more. To say that he would always do that, which is how he felt, and he wanted that to be true. But if he was in Brazil, he wasn't going to be able to drop everything and go running to help her. He couldn't ask his brother Roger to help.

That was his biggest concern. Up until this point, he'd been able to text Ellen any time, call her, and stop in to see her at least every few months. Now, he was facing years potentially without seeing her at all. It was almost more than he could stand.

That alone would be enough to make him decide that he didn't want to go. Except... He knew it would be for the best.

"Travis?"

"Hmm?"

"I'm going to miss you. A lot. Not just because you come save me every time I need you."

He allowed her words to settle deep inside, filling all the spots that longed to stay, to take her hand, to tell her that he loved her and wanted her to wait for him. He couldn't do that. It wasn't right. Although he would wait for her. Faithfully.

"I'm gonna miss you too. I... I know I already said I wouldn't be going if I didn't think it was the right thing to do."

"I know." She didn't say anything more, and they ate in silence. He ate slower than he should have. Because of the storm. He should have hurried, getting out before the snow got any deeper, but he couldn't make himself do that. It was an hour before he pushed away from the counter, their dishes long since washed by Ellen, and stood.

"I better go. Should have left a while ago."

"Be careful." She didn't mention the storm specifically, and he figured that she meant she wanted him to be careful in general, not just tonight.

"I'm always careful."

He gave her a jaunty smile, but she shook her head.

"I mean it. You know I care about you. Please. Be careful."

"For you. I'll be careful." And faithful. "You take care of those pups. I want to see them grown up and trained when I come back."

"They'll be trained and sold before you get back," she said, although the sadness in her voice was covered by a fake happiness she tried to project. But she wasn't fooling anyone, least of all him.

"You be good. I'll see you around," he said, and he smiled at her before he turned around and walked out.

Chapter Four

Ellen looked down at her phone as she parked her car, and sighed. She hadn't seen Travis for five years. He'd gone to Brazil and never come back. During that time, she'd sent him letters, they'd had phone calls and texts, but his job had been very demanding.

Not that she'd been idle, and they hadn't lost touch, they just... hadn't been in contact nearly as much as what she wanted.

But he was on his way home. She thought he was going to make it to the annual Sweet Water spring festival, but he got held up with business. He was tying up all of his loose ends and coming home to stay.

She couldn't wait. Not that Travis was her only friend, even her only good friend. And she didn't expect that things hadn't changed at all. Maybe he'd be bringing a wife home, although if he got married, he'd never told her.

"Are we going in?" her sister Maeve said from the front seat.

Tadgh and Ashley were already in, hanging up decorations and getting things started. They had left Ellen at home to put together a lunch bucket for herself and one for Maeve so they could sell them at the auction.

It was the old-fashioned, buy the bucket and eat with the girl kind of auction. Of course, Tadgh was planning on buying Maeve's bucket. Although Maeve didn't know.

They'd talked about allowing her brother to buy it, and Ellen wasn't entirely sure what they had decided about that other than they thought perhaps Maeve would be disappointed. She had been so excited about getting to put a lunch bucket in the auction.

It was her first auction, and she had made the cookies and the fried apple pies that were in the buckets herself.

Ellen had made country-fried steak again, hoping that it would summon Travis home. Of course, for the last five years, every time she made it she thought of him, but he'd never come. Not that she expected him to, but country-fried steak always made her think of him and long for him to be with her.

Still, the spring festival was one of Ellen's favorites, and she was determined to have a good time. Even if Travis wasn't there to buy her bucket. She would have loved to have been able to sit and catch up with her old friend, but she wasn't going to allow that to spoil the evening for her.

"We sure are, pumpkin," she said to her sister, giving her a smile and sharing an excited look. Maeve wasn't at the age where she was too mature to be called by the nickname that Ellen had given her at birth.

Ellen felt blessed to be able to spend so much time with her sister. Even though she was an adult, with several businesses that she ran on her own, her parents welcomed her, actually wanted her, to continue to live with them. She had never felt like she was in the way or that they were trying to push her out. On the contrary, she felt like they enjoyed her company and wanted her to stay. She loved her family, loved the sense of safety and community that she felt with them, and loved the fact that she had extra years to develop a relationship with her sister.

"Yay!" Maeve said as she grabbed the door handle and pushed the door open.

"Well, well, well, if it isn't Miss Ellen O'Reily." Ellen cringed at the familiar voice. Chalmer Leggins was a familiar sight around town.

He'd graduated with Ellen and had been considered a good athlete. He'd been the high school quarterback, although not good enough to play at the college level, and he hadn't gone to school after his high school career. Instead, he married the head cheerleader, Shanna, and they had two kids together. They'd been divorced for several years, and Chalmer had gotten a job as a truck driver for the Powers family trucking.

Irritatingly, he showed up at a lot of Ellen's dog competition events, and any time she saw him in town, it felt like he chased her down.

She'd been very clear that she wasn't interested, but Chalmer had a hard time taking no for an answer. She had been hoping that he wouldn't be here this evening. Of all the people in town who could buy her basket, Chalmer would be her last choice. Not because she hated him, just because anytime she was even a little bit nice to him, he took it as encouragement and asked her out, not understanding her no and going so far as to show up at her house to pick her up, even after she told him she wasn't interested in going anywhere with him.

"Hi, Chalmer. I'm sorry I can't talk. I need to rush in." They weren't late or anything, she just didn't want to get stuck talking to him.

"No problem. I can walk in with you. I'll carry your bucket."

"No. Actually, it's kind of special, and I don't want it to get upset."

"What? You think I'm not going to be careful enough with your little bucket?" he said, grabbing both buckets out of the back seat and holding them up with one in each hand, held by the handles with his pointer fingers.

Ellen watched with her heart in her throat. Not necessarily for her bucket, but if he did anything to Maeve's bucket, Maeve would be devastated.

"Hey! That's mine. I want to carry it," her little voice chirped up.

"Which one?" he said with a teasing grin that didn't seem friendly. "This one?" He held up the one with the pink flower.

"Yeah. That one's mine."

"If you want it, you need to say the magic word," he said as he slowly began to twist her bucket around on his finger, making slow circles. Ellen resisted the urge to grab for it. That would only make things worse, because it would make Chalmer laugh, and he would continue to tease them. The best thing she could do was to play it cool and not give him the attention and reaction he wanted.

"Please. Please give me my bucket," Maeve said, and she still sounded cheerful, although there was a little wrinkling in her brow that bespoke her concern for her bucket.

Ellen couldn't blame her, she was worried herself. He had started to swing it faster, around his finger, almost as though he were trying to see how fast he could get it to go. Or how long he could do it before they threw a fit and started crying for him to stop.

For Ellen's own bucket, she wouldn't have said a word, but for her sister's bucket, she would give him what he wanted. "That's enough, Chalmer. You're going to spill it."

"Oh, I'm going to spill it," he said in an affected female voice. "Don't you have any faith in me?" He gave her an arrogant look as he began to spin her bucket on his other finger, until he had both buckets going round and round each finger, holding them up and away from his head and body.

"Of course we have faith in you. I'm sure you can spin buckets with the best of them. But we would like to have our meal so that we can go in and put them where they go. We have things to do."

"You're going to drop it," Maeve said, and she no longer sounded happy.

"You're going to drop it," Chalmer mimicked in his affected voice again.

"Chalmer—" Ellen began, but it was too late. He had moved just a little bit, and Maeve's bucket went flying off his finger, smacked into Ellen's car, tipped over, and all the contents ended up on the ground with the bucket on top.

"No!" Maeve let out a keening cry as she dropped to her knees, trying to pick the things up quickly, but the country-fried steak had fallen out of the container and lay on the ground right in the dirt. The mashed potatoes had come to the same fate. She could probably salvage the cookies, although they were cracked, and the pie had broken.

About the only thing that could be salvaged would be the sweet corn cake that had been wrapped in aluminum foil.

Ellen tried to tamp down her anger. Anger never helped anything.

Although, it would certainly make her feel better if she could haul off and smack Chalmer right in the nose.

"Oops," Chalmer said, not sounding sorry at all. Then his brown eyes landed on Ellen. "Maybe the next time I ask you to go out with me, you'll say yes."

"I don't think so," she said, her lips pulled back, but she had them buttoned tightly closed, so she didn't give him a piece of her mind, one that she couldn't afford to lose. She'd never been happy anytime she allowed her mouth to run when it shouldn't, and this would be no different.

"Here. I'll set this one down very, very carefully so that nothing happens to your precious bucket. And I'll make sure I know which one to bid on," he said with a laugh before he slammed her bucket down on the ground and sauntered off.

He was so irritating.

"I'm so sorry about your bucket," Ellen said to Maeve who had touched the country-fried steak that lay on the ground before she realized that there was no way she was going to salvage any of it. "Our buckets were exactly the same other than my blue flowers. Can you salvage your pink flower and put it on my bucket? You can have it."

"Really?" Maeve said, hope entering into her eyes.

"Sure. You made the cookies and the pie for this one just like you did for yours. It's no different."

"I guess you're right. But then you won't have a bucket."

"I'll think of something else to put in the auction," Ellen said, knowing that she had pledged to do something for the auction, and she couldn't go back on her pledge. Well, she could. She could explain what happened. No one was going to hold a gun to her head and make her do it. But she wanted to keep her word. Even when it was hard. Even when she could point to Chalmer as the reason she couldn't.

"But what would you sell?" Maeve asked, and she looked around. "Your car?"

Ellen laughed. "It's a piece of junk, and I can't imagine anyone would want to buy it." It was twenty-five years old, and while it started every time she turned the key, it wasn't much to look at. Which was exactly how she liked it. She'd rather save her money than spend it on a fancy car. Plus, it got good gas mileage, and she wasn't afraid to drive it in the snow, because it didn't matter whether she ran it into a snowbank or not. It already had a lot of dents in it. One more wasn't going to make any difference at all.

"You don't have anything else?" Maeve said, chewing on her lip as they fixed her pink flower beside the blue one that was already on Ellen's bucket.

"I can auction off my clothes," Ellen suggested with a little grin.

"You wouldn't," Maeve said, laughing.

"You're right. I'd better not do that. I might not be welcome at church anymore."

"Church is a hospital for sinners," Maeve said, the pain and suffering that had been in her voice because of Chalmer almost completely gone as they fixed up Ellen's bucket and Ellen handed it to her.

"Thank you. I was really looking forward to this. I've always wanted to have a bucket to sell. I wonder who will buy it?" That was a question Maeve had been asking all day long, and it made Ellen think that there was someone she wanted to buy it.

Maybe one of the Hansom boys. They were a little older than Maeve, but they definitely would catch the girl's eye, although they were a little too wild for Ellen to be comfortable with them.

There were some Powers boys, as well as the Calhoun brothers, two different families of them. Whoever Maeve was interested in was anyone's guess. She was way too young to be dating, but that didn't mean she wasn't looking. Ellen hadn't come right out and asked, and she probably wouldn't. If Maeve wanted to tell her, she certainly could, and Ellen figured she knew that.

Ellen had always been a confidant to her. Every time she had done something wrong and her parents had disciplined her, she cried on Ellen's shoulder, talking about how unfair her life was.

Ellen had tried to gently nudge her in the direction of realizing that her parents were only doing it for her good, the way that Ellen sometimes had to discipline her dogs, for their own good and safety. To turn them into perfectly trained herding animals, who were able to do what they were born to do. Without the training, they might want to chase cows, but that's all they'd do. Just chase them. There would be no rhyme or reason, and they wouldn't be any good to anyone.

Ellen wasn't sure whether Maeve had ever truly understood what she had been trying to say, but she supposed she'd keep trying, until Maeve either got it or moved out.

Maeve carried the bucket with a big smile on her face as she slipped her hand into Ellen's and skipped along beside her as they walked into the community building which had been there for more than a decade. It used to be new, of course, and Ellen still thought of it as new, but a decade had slid by, almost without her recognizing it. She felt like an old lady, because she used to come here as a young girl, about Maeve's age, always excited to be able to participate in whatever town festival was going on. And now, she was part of it.

It was amazing to her how quickly life went by. And a little sad too. She missed being little, the naivety of youth, and the unbridled enthusiasm she had for everything she did. For some reason, there was a growing sadness inside of her, and she wasn't sure exactly what caused it.

It was a longing for something, she supposed, but she wasn't sure what. Maybe it was something that God put in every young person, something that drove them from their comfortable place with their parents and pushed them out into the world, ready to leave their own mark on it.

But she'd think about that some other time, because she loved her town and never wanted to leave, except for that growing discontent inside of her that felt a little bit like wanderlust. Maybe it was just a bit of jealousy because her best friend had been in Brazil for so long and traveled the world, and she barely ever left the town where she grew up.

"We have one lunch bucket for you," Ellen said as they reached the platform and gave Maeve's lunch bucket to the lady in charge.

"You're scheduled for two. Where's the other one?" she said, checking the clipboard that she held in front of her. Every other town in the United States probably had gone electronic, but not Sweet Water.

Ellen didn't smile, because she felt bad. "We dropped one. I'm sorry."

"Well, is there something else you can offer instead?"

"Don't let her offer you her clothes. She told me she wouldn't. Her car is a piece of junk too," Maeve said, with the unfiltered way a child often spoke.

"Thank you for the tips," Lim said, giving a benevolent smile to Maeve. "I would not allow her to offer me her clothes, and I definitely do not want her car. I've seen it. It belongs in a junkyard," Lim added, looking over her glasses.

Ellen tried not to be offended. She loved her car. It was...dependable and had never let her down. Except for the times that she'd run it into a snowbank herself.

But it started when she wanted it to, it ran well, and it got her where she needed to go, without costing her a lot of money. Plus, with all the places that she took her dogs, she really didn't want to get a nice car that would just get covered in dog hair.

But she didn't want to get into an argument with Lim, so she just smiled and held her hands out.

"I wish I could do something. I know I signed up for it." She didn't say what had happened. She wasn't a big believer in offering excuses. Plus, she didn't want to make it sound like she was complaining about Chalmer. This was a party, not the place to complain about people.

"Just sell yourself." Mr. Higginbotham came up beside Lim and spoke over her shoulder.

Chapter Five

"This is a family establishment," Lim said to him with a haughty note in her voice.

Mr. Higginbotham just laughed. "Not like that. My goodness, I don't know why your mind would go there." He looked down his rather generous nose at Lim, giving her a look that said that he was shocked at the filthiness of her mind. "I was just thinking she could be company to whoever buys her for the evening. And she can give them a week's worth of work." He nodded, as though to emphasize his point.

"I don't really have a week to give. I... I do have work I have to do." It was all on her time though. Owning her own business gave her a certain amount of flexibility. As long as the work got done, she could do it whenever she wanted to. Early in the morning, dinnertime, midnight even if she felt like it. But the animals had to be fed, and her dogs had to be trained. The timing was up to her.

"Don't give me that. You still live with your parents, and they'll make sure that you keep your word. Mr. Higginbotham, for once I think you have a good idea." Lim nodded her head and wrote something down on her clipboard.

"Wait a second. I didn't agree to that." Ellen hadn't thought that they were seriously considering this.

"I think you should. After all, you can't shirk your duty." Chalmer walked by, stuck his head in, and made the comment, and Lim nodded in agreement.

Now Ellen wished she would have said something. Because if she said something at this moment, it would really look like sour grapes.

"I'd buy you, but you're rather clumsy," he sneered as he walked off.

Like she'd done anything to him. He'd been the one to be the jerk, and somehow it was her fault. Goodness, she didn't want to get wrapped up with a fellow like that. She had no idea what Shanna had seen in him to begin with.

"I'll offer you last. Just so you know where you are in the program. And thanks again for your basket," Lim said, looking down with a smile at Maeve. "I'm glad that some people keep their word." She shook her head. "You should have been more careful."

Ellen pressed her lips together so she didn't say something unkind.

"She was, but now there are two flowers on mine," Maeve said helpfully, although she didn't mention that the bucket had been Ellen's to begin with.

Ellen didn't want to take that from her either, and if someone was going to have to sell time, it had better be her. She wasn't going to let her sister go to just anyone.

"It's about time you got here!" Jan said, coming over and putting her arm around Ellen's shoulders. "I didn't think you were ever going to show up. We have so much decorating to do. You are helping, right?"

Ellen smiled at her friend. "How about it, Maeve? Are we helping?"

"You betcha!" Maeve said, and then she pointed over to where a group of girls her age, friends from school, were stacking plates and arranging food on the table. "Can I go help them?"

"You sure can. Just be helpful, okay? No goofing off."

"You know I won't. Mom and Dad would be really upset with me if I mess anything up."

Ellen smiled and returned the hug that Maeve gave her before she ran off.

"I can't believe how big she's getting," Ellen said as she watched her sister jog away.

"I can't believe how old you're getting. When are you going to open your eyes and see that there are about seventeen men in this town who would like you to take a second look at them?"

"Seventeen?" Ellen said with a small laugh. "I'm not even sure there's that many men in the whole town."

"Sweet Water is a lot bigger than it used to be. It keeps growing, I think in part because of the Olympic training center. Way back when they put that in, they didn't know how that was going to affect the economy of our little town." She hooked her arm inside of Ellen's, and they started walking toward where the tables were set up. People milled around, since it wouldn't be long until things got started, but they still needed to tape the tablecloths down.

"I guess it's a blessing and a curse," Ellen said, not sure where she fell on the spectrum of loving it or hating it. She loved the town where everyone knew what everyone else was doing, although she didn't like that at the same time. If that were possible. She also loved the small-town familiarity, but having a larger town with more businesses gave a person more options for jobs and economic prosperity, rather than having to move somewhere larger to find a job.

Of course, Ellen could pretty much do her job anywhere she had a pasture for her cows and some way to train her dogs.

But she loved Sweet Water.

"We're going to call it a blessing. Did you hear that they sold the entire Sweet View Ranch complex? And Ford Hansen is one of the major investors. Of course, you probably already know that because he's investing along with Travis Feagley, who's a special friend of yours." Jan wiggled her eyebrows. And then she lowered her voice even more. "I saw him the last time he was back, and he's not a little boy anymore."

"He's not?" Ellen asked, confused. She hadn't thought he'd been home for the five years that he'd been gone, and she didn't understand when Jan had seen him.

"Sure, about a year and a half ago, he showed up. I was in the photography store, framing some pictures, when he walked in and asked where you were."

"Are you sure it was Travis?"

"Sure, he asked about you, then said he was planning on surprising you, but you were out of state at a dog show and were going to be gone for the entire week. So he told me not to tell you that he was there, although I think the statute of limitations has expired on that one, since it was more than a year and a half ago and I heard he's back in town."

Ellen blinked. She hadn't heard that he had visited at all, but it made sense. If he was trying to surprise her and hadn't been able to, then he probably never mentioned it.

"But I'll tell you what, he's filled out since last time I saw him. He was just a string bean before but now, wow. Those wide shoulders, and he's got a man's chest, if you know what I mean."

"Okay," Ellen said, a little unsure. She supposed Jan could have been telling her that Travis was fat, but she didn't think so. She'd find out soon enough. On the one hand, she was glad she didn't know he'd been back and she didn't get to see him. It would have made missing him harder.

If she recalled, that was the big show that Chewy had come in second to her daughter—the pup that was born the night Travis was there to deliver them. Ellen had trained and then sold her, along with her littermates.

It had marked her training as successful, and after that, she had no trouble selling her dogs for a lot of money.

She still got pictures from the family who bought her, a couple in Montana who were using her on their cattle ranch out near Butte.

"Travis said he wasn't going to make it tonight," she murmured as they flattened out the tablecloth and taped it down.

"Oh? That's too bad. I'd heard that country-fried steak was his favorite, and I made that for my bucket. What's in yours?" Jan said with a wink.

Jan, and everyone else in the town, thought Ellen and Travis were just friends. That's what she'd been saying for the last decade. And sometimes she even convinced herself it was true. But the way she felt now, at the idea of Jan fixing a bucket just for Travis, made her feel like maybe he wasn't just a friend to her. After all, Jan was her friend, and she should be happy to see two of her friends get together.

It didn't really make her happy. It made her...jealous.

Maybe that was just because she hadn't seen him for a while and she wanted to spend some time catching up before she had to give him up to someone else. Yeah. That must be it.

It wasn't long after that that they were joined by several other ladies, and the festival started. The auction was first, although they didn't sell the dinner pails until last. There were some craft items and some tools people had donated to raise money for improvements to the sidewalk and the park in town.

Ellen stood in the back, a little nervous. She wished she had fought a little harder to not be in the auction, but she hadn't considered that it might actually be a thing. She never once thought that they would truly auction her off.

Regardless, surely it couldn't be that bad. These were all friends and neighbors, mostly people she knew, although there were some new people in town that she didn't recognize or know well.

There was the family who had bought the Sweet View Ranch. She knew some of them, was friends with Claudia, one of the sisters, but they'd spent a lot of time fixing the ranch up and weren't in town much.

From rumors around town, she knew Travis was involved in it somehow, but she wasn't sure how. She could talk to him about it whenever she saw him again.

Which hopefully would be soon.

She was tempted to pull her phone out and text him, asking when he would be arriving in town, but she didn't. Something must have held him up, but as long as he wasn't in any danger, she realized that was just the nature of his business.

It was the thing that had kept them apart for the last five years. Although, knowing that he had been in town and wanted to surprise her had made her sad. Even though she was glad that a puppy she had bred had won that dog show, and her business had benefited from it, she would give that up in a heartbeat in order to see her friend.

"And, ladies and gentlemen, we have one last thing to auction off. Ellen?" announced Mr. Higginbotham, the auctioneer. She supposed that was her cue.

Wishing she'd been standing closer to the front so she didn't have to walk the entire length of the building, she started up the aisle.

Maybe to fill in the time, or maybe he really wanted the audience to be well-informed, Mr. Higginbotham started talking about her.

"You guys all know Ellen. She grew up in town. Tadgh and Ashley are her parents, and they're well respected in town. You guys all know that Ellen is a hard worker, and I'm sure we've all seen her around with her cow Daisy and her dog Chewy."

She felt like she was still thirteen, rather than twenty-three. Maybe that was how the town saw her, with her dog and cow. Maybe if she wanted to catch a certain man's eye, she should start being a little more feminine.

It was always interesting to see how people saw her, she supposed. But she didn't know what she expected. They saw what she presented, and that was exactly right.

"She had promised to donate a lunch for the auction, and she came here empty-handed, so this is what we do with people who don't do what they say they're going to do."

She felt like that was a little unfair. She'd gotten her lunch to the parking lot. If it wasn't for Chalmer, she would have her lunch in the building too.

Seemed like Chalmer should be the one on the chopping block for that, but she took the criticism silently. Maybe someday things would get straightened out. She often wondered if she'd get to heaven and God would fix everything. All the unfairly accused people would finally be vindicated, lies would come to light, and the truth would be known.

Maybe she was wrong about that, but she couldn't help but remember that Jesus was led as a lamb to slaughter, and he didn't open his mouth to defend himself. If Jesus was her example, shouldn't she do the same?

It had been a question she'd been thinking about for a while, and she'd been trying to practice just allowing things to slide, rather than fighting them and spending a lot of time trying to prove she was right. It seemed like she wasted a lot of time trying to defend herself at times, when it really didn't matter.

"So, Ellen has agreed to donate the rest of this evening, and a week's worth of time, eight hours a day, for five days, to whoever bids the highest for her. Now, you can put her to work, or you can put her in the parlor and look at her, but no touching. And I have it on good authority that she's not allowed to take any clothes off."

There were a few gasps and a lot of chuckles from the audience as he said that.

Ellen could feel her cheeks flaming, clear up to the tips of her ears.

This was not her idea of a good time, although she did feel like the money was going to a good cause.

She had enjoyed the rest of the auction, watching as ladies stood by their buckets, and she'd been happy for Maeve as Tadgh had bought her bucket.

Maeve had beamed and walked away hand in hand with her dad.

It had been adorable, and Ellen had smiled the whole time.

Hers was probably not going to have such a happy ending. But there was no law that said she had to be bought by a man. Maybe one of the aquatic ladies would buy her, and they'd end up doing eight hours of water instruction.

It was kind of crazy that Ellen had gotten roped into being the aquatic instructor. She really wasn't that great of a swimmer, but they'd needed an instructor, and someone had asked her, and she said sure.

She ended up learning right along with the ladies, but they had fun, and she supposed that was the most important thing after getting out and being active for them.

Regardless, she could keep her hopes up that that would be what would happen. She wouldn't mind that at all.

Swallowing hard, she walked up the steps and stood on the stage.

"Come on, girl, come a little closer. I'm not going to bite you," Mr. Higginbotham said, making her feel like she was three.

She walked closer, feeling like she was headed to the gallows. Reminding herself that the people watching were her friends, her family, and her neighbors.

She shouldn't have any reason to be afraid. Maybe she wasn't exactly afraid, she just was...nervous. She'd never done anything like this before, never known anyone who had. Couldn't really believe that it was happening, even as Mr. Higginbotham started the bidding at a dollar.

She almost gave him a second look. Really? A dollar for an evening and five working days? That didn't seem like nearly enough.

Someone called out ten dollars, and then fifty, and the bidding went up from there. It was happening too fast for Ellen to be able to tell exactly who was bidding. She caught her uncle Tadgh's smirk as he bid sixty-two dollars and then waved a hand saying it was too high after the next bid, and everyone around him laughed.

She smirked as well. Since she knew he was just messing with her.

Then, as the bidding went over a hundred dollars, she heard a voice that made her cringe.

Chalmer's voice. She hadn't even considered that someone like him might buy her. She had been more focused about actually standing up here and offering herself for sale.

No one seemed worried about it, and Chalmer wasn't known as a bad person. He had two small children with Shanna, his ex-wife, and he treated them well. It just seemed that he was a little pushy when it came to Ellen. Although she had never complained to anyone, so no one would think to stop him from purchasing her.

Not that she thought she was going to be in any danger. She just wouldn't enjoy her forced time of servitude if Chalmer was the one who would be telling her what to do.

But as the price went up, there were three or four different voices, and always Chalmer's rang in when Ellen's hope started to rise that he would be outbid.

Finally, when the price was almost two hundred dollars, which was high for the working folk of Sweet Water, Mr. Higginbotham looked around and said, "Going once, going twice..." He paused for dramatic effect probably, and Ellen stood with her heart in her throat.

Chalmer's bid had been the last one.

"Sold!" He slammed his gavel down on the podium and then used it to point out Chalmer. "There you go. You won the little lady, but she doesn't come with food."

The crowd laughed as Ellen lifted her chin, smiled a little for the benefit of the crowd, and then lifted a shoulder. She actually *had* come with food, and it was Chalmer's fault that she didn't at this point. She kind of felt like it was almost just desserts.

But she would never say that.

Chalmer grinned. "Guess you get the pleasure of my company after all," he said with a smile that Ellen supposed could have been called charming, but it just looked sinister to her.

"I guess I do," she said, knowing she sounded lame but not knowing what else to say. It wasn't like she was excited about it, or happy. It was one of those things in life that she was going to have to endure, and she also made a mental note to pack a spare bucket the next time she came to one of these things. Of course, he was just as likely to spill two as he was to spill one.

"Come on, we'll go outside. It's less crowded out there, and we'll have more privacy."

"You gotta feed the girl," someone called out as he grabbed a hold of Ellen's elbow. She didn't pull it out of his hand; she didn't want to be rude. But this was not the way she had expected her evening to go. Being bought was one thing, then being led away from everyone else while they all laughed and enjoyed each other's company around the tables that had been set up inside for that very purpose was something completely different.

It wasn't like she desired to have any kind of time alone with Chalmer.

But when Mr. Higginbotham had offered her, it was her giving her time for someone else. She wasn't supposed to be demanding her way.

Trying to play along with the spirit of things, Ellen walked beside Chalmer as he called over his shoulder, "That's fine, I got us some hot wings and some of Lucinda's mincemeat. That will tide us over."

Ellen tried not to groan. Mrs. Bothim had made the hot wings, and they were extremely hot. If she wanted to have pain while she ate, she supposed spicy food would hit the spot, but she didn't deliberately seek out pain on purpose and had a hard time understanding people who did. Not that she would judge, just a personal preference on her part. And mincemeat was her absolute least favorite kind of pie. She didn't even really consider it pie. It was more like...she wasn't even sure.

But she'd been raised to be thankful for what she had, and laughing a little to herself at the way her evening had gone completely off the rails, she allowed Chalmer to lead her by the elbow to the door.

He opened it, and they walked out into the dusty twilight. Ellen tried not to show the longing she felt to stay inside, especially as she heard Mr. Higginbotham say, "Oh, look at this. We found a couple more buckets that need to be auctioned off. All right, if you put your big checkbook away, you need to get it back out."

Chapter Six

"Travis!" Mr. Higginbotham said as Travis walked in the community center door. Travis turned his head to the stage where Mr. Higginbotham stood with a makeshift microphone, which always made his voice sound tinny, holding up a pail that had been beautifully decorated with loads of flowers and material and other knickknacks. "You're here just in time. This is our last meal. If you want something to eat, you better pony up."

"Is it Ellen's?" he called back, grinning so that everyone would know that he was mostly joking.

He wasn't, actually. He really wanted to know if it was Ellen's, because he'd come as fast as he could, hoping that he'd be able to make it in time to bid on her bucket. He hadn't thought he was going to make it, and he had told her so, not wanting her to have her hopes up and to let her down.

It had been five years since he'd seen her, and while they spent some time texting and facetiming, it wasn't like seeing someone in person.

He couldn't wait.

But his chest deflated when Mr. Higginbotham shook his head. "Beggars can't be choosy. The bid's at ten bucks. Give me eleven, Travis. And we'll welcome you back."

He grinned and lifted his shoulder. If it was the last bucket, he wasn't going to get to eat with Ellen. She was already eating with someone else, and his eyes swept the room, trying to figure out where she was. He looked up and down the tables but didn't see her distinctive auburn hair.

No one else bid on the bucket, and he got it for the eleven dollars. It was a good thing, he supposed, since he hadn't been paying attention to the auction and had no thought to bid again if he needed to.

"All right, Travis, come on up here, pay for your food, and get your girl."

Travis turned, pulling his eyes away from the tables, still not seeing Ellen, and took one step toward the stage when his heart quit beating.

Shanna. She stood on stage, taking her bucket from Mr. Higginbotham with a happy smile as her two children stood around her legs, and Mr. Higginbotham handed it to her and nodded at Travis.

Shanna sent a knowing look in his direction, and Travis tried to return her smile. He'd avoided her as much as he could since he figured out exactly what was going on with her in high school. She was just using him. But high school was a long time ago, and surely he could have a civil meal with her now. Even if he would have preferred to be with Ellen.

Sometimes things just didn't work out the way a person wanted them to, and this was one of those times, he thought as he pulled eleven bucks out of his wallet and gave it to the lady at the table who was collecting the money.

Why couldn't Ellen's bucket have been last?

She probably would have made sure that it would have been if she had known that he was coming, if he hadn't sent that text that said that he wasn't going to make it, because he didn't want to disappoint her.

It was always easier to see what a person should have done than what a person should do.

Regardless, he turned toward Shanna, who stood at his elbow, and then looked down at the two small children beside her.

"I've heard you had some kids," he said by way of greeting.

"And hello to you too," she said, wrinkling her nose at him and giving him a sultry smile. At least he assumed that was what kind of smile it was. It was the kind of smile that a woman gave a man when she wanted him to know that she was interested in him. He'd picked that much up along with all the other things that Ford had taught him.

But he'd always been faithful to Ellen. He supposed he always would be. Except, he kind of expected her to come over and greet him when she saw him walk in.

"I guess we ought to go find a seat," he said, feeling a little more comfortable now that he was twenty-eight instead of eighteen. That was one thing that Ford's training had done, given him confidence. Confidence that he sorely lacked when he was a kid.

Not that he thought that he could handle a woman like Shanna, and he definitely didn't want to fool himself into believing that. She could make shark bait out of him, and well he knew it. But he wasn't the insecure kid he used to be, either. The one who just wanted to fit in and who fell for sultry smiles and a come-hither look from someone who was older and more popular than he was.

He took the bucket from her, careful not to brush her fingers, but offered her his arm, figuring it was the right thing to do.

"Oh. So gallant," she said, batting her eyes again.

He kind of thought she might introduce him to her kids, but she didn't. "Let's go outside. It's so hot in here," she said, fanning herself and blowing out a breath like she truly was warm.

Travis didn't want to go anywhere, and he supposed he could tell her that he'd rather sit at the tables, but it might be easier for her kids if they didn't have to be confined. Maybe there were other people who had figured the same thing and would be outside too so they wouldn't be completely alone.

"It's been so long since I've seen you. You've definitely grown up. Look at those shoulders," she said, and her frank appraisal made him uncomfortable, despite the fact that he considered himself much more capable and confident than he used to be.

Shanna reminded him of a shark even more than she used to. Which was particularly unsettling considering that her children were standing right beside them.

"So what are your kids' names?" he asked, hoping to divert her attention. A mother loved talking about her children, right? He knew that wasn't necessarily true, since his own mother had not particularly cared one way or the other about him or his two brothers. Which, with the insight that hindsight gave, probably turned out to benefit him.

If his mother had cared about him, Ford Hansen might not have taken him under his wing, and Travis might not have been given the opportunities that he had been. He wouldn't be twenty-eight, with enough money in the bank to purchase his own ranch out of pocket, as well as investing in a property and family that was going to benefit the entire community, if he and Ford had figured right.

"Enzo and Atlas," she said, and her tone was dismissive. It reminded him a good bit of his mother's voice when she talked about her children. Maybe that wasn't fair, since his mother had been an alcoholic and an occasional-to-often drug user as well. As far as he knew, that did not describe Shanna, although he hadn't been in town for five years, and a lot could have changed in that time.

"Hey there, guys," he said, assuming those were boys' names. He wasn't quite sure from the length of the hair on both of the kids what gender they were. It used to be it wasn't hard to tell, but nowadays, it was dangerous to make an assumption.

She didn't say which one was which, but the smaller one hid further behind her leg while Shanna used her hand to try to drag him away from her and make him walk beside her. She yanked on it a bit, and Travis cringed.

He didn't have any experience with small children, other than raising his brothers, who weren't that much younger than him, and he couldn't remember how they were at that age.

Of course, Ellen's sister and brother were exceptions. He'd been around her, and them, but he'd never watched them without Ellen.

Kids were a mystery to him, as were women for the most part. He'd kept his nose to the grindstone and learned what he could about business, keeping his thoughts focused on Ellen any time he was tempted to think about a woman, and he had to admit, that was quite often.

Opening the door, he held it while Shanna gave him one last grin and then swept through, practically dragging her child behind her while the other one tripped at her heels.

He walked out into the dark night, the air cool, but not cold. Although, coming from Brazil, where he'd been, he was used to subtropical weather. North Dakota would take a bit of getting used to again, but he was happy to be home.

Not quite as happy as he had intended to be, because he had expected his evening was going to be spent with Ellen, not Shanna.

"We'll just go over here," Shanna said, walking confidently toward the swing set and picnic table that sat beside it.

"I said no!"

A woman's voice carried clearly over the night air, and Travis stopped as the hair on the back of his head lifted. That sounded like Ellen.

"I heard you, and I just figured you didn't really mean it."

"I meant it. We're not going to have this argument every day. You can get that straight right now."

"You're mine, fair and square."

"I know, but there are certain things even you cannot get away with."

He was sure it was Ellen's voice. He didn't recognize the man, but from the conversation it sounded like...Ellen was married? How else could she be "his?"

But wouldn't Ellen have told him if she'd gotten married?

He stopped thinking about that as he heard a bit of a scuffle. Forgetting completely about Shanna, he turned toward the source of the voices.

"Let go!" It was Ellen's voice again.

"We're gonna get this straight right now," the man's voice said, and far from the indulgent tones of earlier, he sounded angry, threatening.

That made Travis walk faster, and their shapes came into sight.

There was a pole light as a backdrop, so there was a good bit of shadow, but there was no doubt it was Ellen, and while he knew that this was not a place for her to bring her dog, he was slightly surprised that Chewy wasn't there. This wouldn't be happening if Chewy had been around. Chewy was not an aggressive dog, but she would absolutely not allow a strange man to take hold of her mistress like that. Except, maybe Chewy didn't regard him as a strange man. Maybe

Chewy knew exactly who this man was. If it was the way it sounded, and he was Ellen's...husband.

How could she do this to him? How could she get married without even saying anything? His heart squeezed as he thought about all the dreams he'd dreamed about the two of them together.

He thought that he'd been clear about what his intentions were, but it had been ten years ago, and he hadn't even seen her for five. She didn't know that he had come home a year and half ago to see her.

He must have misunderstood when she told him, because he thought the trials were in Sweet Water, and he hadn't realized she was traveling for them. He didn't have the time to follow her and had left without ever telling her he'd shown up for them and to see her. They had coincided with a week that he had to be in the states, but unfortunately, he had business he had to take care of too and couldn't stay around.

Sometimes those things happened, but he'd been bitterly disappointed. So disappointed that he ended up never even mentioning it to Ellen. He felt like an idiot, knowing he must have misheard, and he also didn't want to admit how much he wanted to see her.

Now that he was listening to her and thinking that he'd missed his opportunity, he wished he would have said something, even if it felt like too big of a risk to take or not the right time. At least this pain in his heart wouldn't be so debilitating.

But, husband or no, that man had no right to treat her like that. Travis stepped closer.

"Listen here, you might think you're all high and mighty, but you're mine, fair and square, and it's about time you started acting like it." The man yanked on Ellen's arm, eliciting a gasp of pain from her.

"She said no."

Travis stepped into the circle of light, knowing that it shone directly on his face, while theirs were still in shadow, as the man's head jerked to look toward him.

"Get out of here. This is not your business."

"She said no," he said again, firmly. Letting the man know that he wasn't backing down.

"Travis?" Ellen said, a question at first, but then a smile spread over her face. And Travis almost forgot that she was standing beside her husband, who was insisting that she was his, and that she needed to act the part, or whatever he was doing.

It was enough to see her smile, to see the happiness that seeing him brought her. To feel his own happiness bubbling in his soul, although it was tempered and then almost extinguished when he remembered that she was married. He was the one who had insisted that they had to be friends. This was all his fault.

"Travis!" Shanna's voice came from behind him, sharp and annoyed. "You were supposed to follow me over to the picnic table. The kids are playing on the swing set. Get over here."

He ignored her. The man still had not let go of Ellen's arm. Irritation made Travis's fingers itchy.

"Oh my goodness! I thought you weren't going to make it!" Ellen said, and there was nothing but joy in her voice. No concern for the man holding her, no irritation, nothing except perfect happiness that he was standing in front of her. It was exactly what he would have expected from her, except what about the man?

"He didn't buy you, I did. You're staying beside me." The man spat onto the blacktop and did not let go of Ellen as she pulled, like she was going to walk toward Travis.

He bought her?

Had Ellen gotten into some kind of financial difficulty? That was so weird. Surely if she had been, he would be the first person that she'd have talked to. Her uncle could have helped, too; she wouldn't have needed to sell herself... That was so...centuries outdated. Or maybe he was just confused.

"You don't own me. That's not what that meant."

"It meant what I say it does. You obey me."

Travis's brows went up. A lot of women talked about taking the obey out of the marriage vows, and he always thought that that was un-biblical. After all, the biblical command was to obey. It was there in black and white. It wasn't that he was trying to lord it over anyone, and it actually made him feel a little uncomfortable to think that his wife was supposed to obey him, like there was something special about him that made him worth obeying. But he wasn't the Creator, he was just the creature, and to question that would be to effectively say that he knew better than God. Which he absolutely did not.

Regardless, it wasn't really his concern, and with the pain in his heart, he was almost tempted to walk away. But he could not allow a man to treat a woman like that, whether they were married or not. Although what Ellen was doing with this person, Travis did not understand. How could she have thought it was a good idea to get married to someone like that?

Maybe he had just been a very good actor while they were dating.

"It meant no such thing," Ellen said, and she sounded angrier than he'd ever heard her, even though her voice had not been raised. "Let go of my arm. Or I will walk right back in that building and make this null and void."

"You can't. You agreed to it."

"I agreed to spend the evening with you and to spend five eight-hour days with you. Doing what you want, without you touching me. Don't you remember that part?"

"No. I don't." He sneered at her, and it was obvious to Travis that he obviously did remember, he just chose to ignore it.

"The lady said unhand her."

"What are you gonna do about it?" Chalmer said.

Uh oh. That was a good question. What was he going to do about it? Travis couldn't remember the last time he'd gotten into a fight. It had been a decade.

Back in the day, he'd been a bit of a brawler, although he'd never been any good at it. He'd had a temper, a chip on his shoulder, and thought the world was against him. Ford had fixed all of that, but maybe he fixed it a little too well, considering that the idea of fighting about anything was distasteful. But the man wasn't going to manhandle Ellen. Plus, as he thought about it, he realized that they must not be married. She said something about five days, eight hours.

"You guys aren't married?" he said, figuring that probably should have been his first question.

Chapter Seven

"Travis! Ew!"

"I was married to that jerkface, and only a fool would do that again." Shanna's voice came from behind him. He'd heard that she got married, but he hadn't known to whom, only that they had a couple of kids and got divorced. And he thought that information came from one of his brothers, not Ellen. She didn't typically relay the gossip in town when they talked. She talked more about her animals, what was happening on the farm, her ideas and things she hoped to do, and she seemed very interested in what was going on with him.

"Shut up. Who asked you anyway?" The man spat in Shanna's direction.

"Let go," Ellen said to him, tugging on her arm. She said it in a low voice, like she was appeasing everyone, and Travis hid a smile. If the man hadn't been so annoying, he probably wouldn't have. But he was guessing that Ellen just wanted him to let go so Travis wouldn't end up in a fight. He could almost hear her saying it now.

"I'm not letting go. You're coming with me. It's too crowded around here," he said and started dragging Ellen away.

Travis hesitated for just a second. Maybe a split second. He wasn't going to allow that man to drag his best friend away. Was he?

He didn't know how else to stop it, other than to take three large strides forward, grab the man's shoulder, spinning him around, and growl, "Let go of her."

At least he was holding onto her with his right hand, so if they were going to fight, assuming the man was right-handed, he would have to let go of Ellen first.

"Get ready to duck, kiddo," he said to Ellen.

"Travis," she said with a warning note in her voice, and Travis wasn't sure whether it was because he called her kiddo, which she didn't really like, or whether it was because she didn't want him to get into a fight, which he didn't really have a choice about.

He didn't take his eyes off the man in front of him to try to figure out which thing Ellen meant.

"Chalmer, let me go. Travis is a lot bigger than you are."

Travis didn't think he was any bigger than Chalmer. In fact, Chalmer definitely outweighed him. They were about the same height, though.

Chalmer sneered. "That toothpick? He's not bigger than me."

Maybe Ellen was just trying to convince Chalmer that he was going to lose the fight. Travis couldn't be sure who would win, but he couldn't not do something.

"He'll go down with the first swing," the man said, grinning for one second before his grin faded, his eyes narrowed, and he swung at Travis as hard as he could.

Travis was not expecting it. He was more concerned about telling Ellen to get out of the way. He had his mouth open when Chalmer hit him square in the jaw.

The blow felt like a sledgehammer hitting him in the face. Travis stumbled back. Immediately something warm and wet started running down his face, and the world seemed to dip and sway and get black or red, he couldn't really tell what color it was. He felt dizzy, like he was going to fall down at any second.

But in some subconscious quarter of his brain, he knew he couldn't just walk away and tend to his wounds. He needed to fight back. He must have been softer than what he realized, because the temptation to just sit down and hold his head in his hand for a few seconds was strong.

But he couldn't do that and risk Chalmer grabbing Ellen and walking away with her. The only witness was Shanna, and she didn't seem to be the slightest bit concerned about Ellen's safety. Nor did she seem to care about anything other than the fact that he hadn't listened to her and followed her across the parking lot.

So he stepped forward, his eyes on Chalmer as he smirked.

He tried to channel his fighting days from high school as Chalmer faked a jab with his left before powering forward with his right hand.

That time, Travis was ready, or maybe Chalmer's aim was a little bit off, because the blow glanced off his shoulder, and he was able to get in a blow of his own, hitting Chalmer in the jaw with a satisfying thud that jerked his head around. It also sent sharp arrows of pain from his knuckles up his arm and out his shoulder. He had forgotten that punching someone hurt that bad. It almost felt like he hit a tooth.

Chalmer recovered much faster than Travis and came back, this time with a fake right and a hook with his left, while he threw a leg out to kick, aiming for Travis's groin, probably just for good measure.

It was more than Travis could fend off, but considering that he already felt dizzy and a little confused, the blows didn't have quite the same effect the first one did. The left hook caught him in the stomach, but not a solid blow, and Chalmer's foot hit him in the thigh, rather than its intended target.

He was able to get two good hits in on Chalmer's face and one in his stomach as he vaguely realized that someone was screaming and someone else was shouting. Women, it sounded like, although he didn't stop to try to figure out what they were saying. Instead, he hit Chalmer again, and that time, the man dropped to the pavement, groaning.

"That's enough, Travis," Ellen said, walking toward him and touching his forearm lightly with her fingers.

"Sorry," he said. Not sure what he was apologizing for, but feeling like he needed to do it anyway. Maybe it was the look on her face. Did she look disappointed?

"What was going on?" he said, wiping the back of his hand across his face and seeing blood come off on his wrist.

"It's a long story, but he bought me at the auction. I was supposed to spend the evening with him, and give him five days this week. Not for anything inappropriate, just...work or company or something like that."

"He wasn't to grab a hold of you."

"No."

"Come on. We're going in to lodge a complaint, and I'll buy him out."

"Travis. I'm not a possession."

"I know." He stopped moving and focused his eyes on her. Of course he knew. How could she think otherwise? Their eyes met, and the fun and camaraderie that normally lay between them wasn't there. Something else seemed to shimmer in the air instead. Something a lot more serious. Something that reminded him of the night that he left ten years ago, when they'd been in the barn together.

It felt warm and dangerous and he had to shake his head, because this was not the time or the place. Behind him, Shanna said something, although she had to repeat herself before he heard it.

"Where are you going? We're supposed to be eating together. Did you forget about me, hello?!"

Chalmer groaned, and Travis looked at him on the blacktop. He didn't want to hurt the man. But Chalmer had thrown the first punch. Surely that would count for something, although he had to admit he was definitely out of practice when it came to knowing what the law said about fistfights anymore.

"I think he's going to be okay," Ellen said softly, looking from Chalmer to Travis and lifting her hand to touch his face with the tips of her fingers. "I suppose you will be too, but I think it's gonna look worse before it looks better." Her hand seemed to linger for a moment, and Travis held his breath, content to allow her soft touch, not wanting anything else more than he wanted Ellen, whatever he could get from her.

"Let's go get this taken care of," he said softly, not wanting to move but not able to stand the idea of Ellen being in Chalmer's "possession" for another minute.

"Travis."

He stared down at her. "Please."

At that word, he could see her resolve melt away. It almost made him smile the way she capitulated. Her shoulders lowered and her head nodded, even though her lips were flat.

"What about me?" Shanna said from his other side.

"I'll be back in a minute. Walk over to the swing set where your kids are."

"You promise?" she asked, and while her voice was shrill and almost shrew-like, he detected a note of insecurity underneath it. He figured that all along Shanna had been insecure, and here he thought he had been that one. But sometimes people covered their insecurities with a lot of bluster and bluff.

Very seldom, at least what he had found, was that people were rotten to the core. There was almost always good mixed in with the bad, some kind of redeeming features. After all, humans were created in God's image. God loved them, so there had to be something there to love.

It wasn't his job to figure Shanna out though. His concern was for his friend, and he looked back at Ellen.

She still had her lips pulled back, but she fell into step beside him as he started toward the door. He opened it, and she walked through. The bright light gave him an almost instant headache, but no one looked in their direction as he strode in. It hadn't been that long since he walked out; Mr. Higginbotham and the lady at the table who had taken the money were still conferring together. Probably totaling up the amounts.

He walked straight to the table.

"I'd like to pay for Ellen. Whatever Chalmer paid for her, I'll double it."

They looked up, and the woman gasped. "What happened to you?"

"You can't pay for her. You already bought a lunch bucket. You can't have two."

"Technically, I didn't come with a lunch bucket, remember?" Ellen spoke, and Travis was grateful. His brain still wasn't processing at its normal speed. "It was just me."

That made Mr. Higginbotham close his mouth, and then he nodded. "I guess you're right. Although, the spirit of the law would be that you can't have two, but... I suppose that there isn't anything specifically saying that you can't purchase someone's bucket and also purchase a person." He smirked a little before his eyes went back to Travis's face. But the man didn't say anything about it.

"What about Chalmer? Is he going to be okay with that?" the lady asked, apparently deciding that she wasn't going to say anything more about his face, either. Maybe it didn't look as bad as it felt. Which was pretty bad. Although the headache was much worse.

"He was trying to drag her away, and she was saying no. He wouldn't listen."

"Is that so?" Mr. Higginbotham said.

"That's terrible," the lady said.

"It's true," Ellen confirmed, like they needed a witness.

"So, he didn't agree to sell her to you?"

"No. I'm demanding that I buy her. Because she is not going back out with a man who won't listen to her when she says no."

The lady nodded her head firmly, but Mr. Higginbotham appeared slightly reluctant. He was a stickler for the rules, probably didn't care as much about the personal side of things. A typical man, perhaps.

Travis could see himself being the same way, and he hoped he wasn't.

"All right then. If that's the way it is, Chalmer has forfeited his right to this purchase, if he couldn't obey the basic laws of assault."

Ellen nodded slowly, although he could see her cringing a little at the idea that Mr. Higginbotham was calling what had happened an assault. Chalmer had assaulted Travis. He wasn't quite sure that Ellen would agree that he had also assaulted her.

But maybe Ellen didn't understand how quickly the situation could have escalated with her defying Chalmer.

In Brazil, things were a little looser, and Travis had experienced how quickly a man's temper could escalate and all of the terrible results that could occur. Not often, but enough to know that Ellen was probably in more danger than what she thought she was.

"All right, it's changed," the woman said and then named the sum that Travis owed.

He pulled the money out of his pocket, thankful that he typically kept a little cash in his wallet for emergencies. This was definitely something he would term an emergency.

"Thank you," Ellen said as Travis nodded his head and echoed her words of appreciation.

"You probably ought to get that looked at," the woman said, nodding at Travis's face.

"Maybe I'll assign that task to my new servant," he said, some of the tension and anger draining out of him at the fact that it was done and Ellen was out of harm's way.

"Are you serious?" she said under her breath, annoyance and affection and amusement all evident in her tone.

He smiled at the contradictions. It was just like Ellen. Only, now that he had a chance to really look at her, she was all grown up. So much more mature than last time he had seen her in person. He couldn't believe how much older she looked. Not old as in decrepit, but old as in mature. She didn't look like a young girl anymore, she looked like a woman. How could he have been gone so long and thought that nothing would change?

"You're not married, right?" He remembered his fears from earlier, and the question came out unbidden.

"What made you ask that?"

"Some things that you and Chalmer were saying made me feel like maybe you had gotten married and not talked to me about it first."

"Come on. That would never happen."

She gave him a look that made him feel like he was being ridiculous. Maybe he was. But the look also made him feel like maybe she hadn't considered him for a marriage partner. Just that she would tell him if she did. That wasn't exactly what he wanted to hear.

"You go on outside. Shanna is expecting you. I'm going to go get some ice."

What was that in her tone? She sounded a little...annoyed?

Maybe she was annoyed that instead of having a nice conversation with him, she was going to be fixing up his face. He wasn't sure. Regardless, he said, "Do you think you can get yourself outside without some other dude trying to drag you off?"

"You know, in all my life, I've never had a problem with men wanting to drag me off somewhere. Figures you'd walk in on the night where that suddenly became an issue."

"I think maybe you just have never noticed."

She laughed. "I don't think so. But if you want to phrase it that way, I guess I'm not going to argue with you."

"I'm glad I walked in when I did," he said, his eyes serious.

Some of the amusement faded out of her face as she nodded in agreement. "Me too." Then she smiled again, but it didn't seem to reach her eyes. "Go on. I'm coming."

He jerked his head up, still watching her, because she just wasn't acting quite right, and he knew that once they went out with Shanna, he wouldn't have a chance to ask her about it. But she turned and started walking away before he could say anything, and so he walked outside, determined that whatever it took, he would get to the bottom of it.

Chapter Eight

Ellen put a hand on the freezer and tried to still her trembling fingers. Her whole body felt like Jell-O. She had been scared to death that Travis was going to get hurt. He didn't even seem to hear her calling for him to stop, but she'd shut her mouth after he'd been able to get himself up enough to block Chalmer's punch and get in one of his own. She'd been terrified that something was going to happen to him after he had finally returned after five years away.

Then, after Chalmer was on the ground, and they'd gone inside to get things with her straightened out, it finally hit her that he bought Shanna's lunch bucket. It was like high school all over again.

But he'd insisted they should just be friends. And she'd honored that, although she hoped for more all the time. He promised he was going to kiss her. But apparently it was Shanna that he had been pining for, since the night he got home, he was already eating supper with her.

She tried to swallow the feeling of bitter disappointment. Push aside her heartbreak.

"Are you okay?" a voice asked from behind her. The general murmur and laughter of the townsfolk was muted in the kitchen, although she could still hear them. The hustle and bustle that would have been going on earlier as everyone grabbed food and drinks and got

59

seated had died down, and the kitchen had been deserted. At least she thought it had been.

She turned around to see one of the Clyborne sisters, Claudia. Claudia was about the same age as she was, and they had become good friends since Claudia had moved in with her family. They bought the Sweet View Ranch complex outside of town and, with the help of a few anonymous investors, hoped to make the ranch a roaring success and bring even more commerce dollars into Sweet Water.

The family was an asset to Sweet Water, although Ellen didn't know them all well. Claudia had been kind, and Ellen considered her a friend.

"I'm fine."

"You look white as a sheet, and your fingers are trembling." Claudia lifted her brows, but her voice was gentle. She wasn't accusing, she was asking. Stating what she saw and then inviting Ellen to tell her what the issue was if Ellen so chose. Ellen appreciated the fact that she wasn't trying to force her way into Ellen's life.

But at the same time, she really wanted to tell someone. Or at least talk to someone. Maybe not bare her heart. Could she?

"You saw Chalmer buy me."

"Yeah, I felt bad for you. If I had had more money on me, I would have bought you myself. It didn't say that it had to be a man."

"No. And that would have been a relief, trust me."

"Yeah, I'm sure. I was sitting there thinking to myself that I was really glad that I had brought a lunch bucket to put on auction, because if I hadn't, and they sold me... I don't know if I would have gone through with it."

"I didn't want to. But honestly, I didn't really think they would force me to do it. I guess I could have insisted, but it would have been a scene. And I'm not very good at that."

"I know. You're so sweet. That's not necessarily a bad thing, it's just I can see how they would have railroaded you into it before you even realized it."

"Yeah. That's exactly what happened."

"So it didn't go well?" Claudia raised her brows.

"No. You could say that." Ellen laughed a bit, and Claudia looked intrigued.

"Spill," she commanded.

Ellen sighed, opening up the freezer and getting the ice tray out before going to the drawer looking for a Ziploc bag as she spoke.

"Chalmer grabbed a hold of me and wouldn't let go. I told him no, told him to let go, but he didn't listen."

"And that's where you popped him in the face. And then ran screaming for your life," Claudia said firmly and with a little heat.

"I was getting ready to do that. He's bigger than I am but not as big as my cows. If I can manhandle them, I figured I could handle him, at least enough to get away."

"I'm glad you got away... You did get away, right?" Claudia's voice held compassion and concern again, and Ellen nodded immediately. She didn't want Claudia to think the worst.

"Yes. That's why I'm getting this ice," she said as she filled the bag up with cubes before putting the tray back in the freezer. "Travis came. And he and Chalmer fought."

"Really? You had two men fighting over you?"

"Not really. Travis is just a friend, and he heard me tell Chalmer no, and he was just making sure the guy listened."

"Well, that sounds like about what you need to do to make sure that Chalmer listens, only take a sledgehammer to the hardest head in Sweet Water."

"Yeah. I don't know how Shanna managed to stay with him for as long as she did."

"Shanna gets what she deserves, from what I can see," Claudia said with a little bit of irony in her tone.

"That's possible. Travis bought her bucket though. And they're eating together."

"Then she should be the one in here fixing ice for him," Claudia said, laughing a bit, and Ellen wasn't sure that she could tell Claudia that...she didn't want Shanna fixing Travis up. She didn't want Shanna anywhere near Travis.

"Travis is my friend. I don't mind helping him at all or giving him ice which is probably all I'm going to do. But... I guess I want someone better for him than Shanna."

"Oh. I see. Yeah, from what I've heard about Travis, he could do a lot better too. He apparently has been quite successful since he left Sweet Water. I've never met him, but if he's your friend, he must be a good man."

"Oh my goodness. Yeah. He's definitely a good man."

Travis was better than good, but she couldn't really gush on about him without Claudia thinking things that probably were true. Or maybe they were a little bit true. That Ellen cared a lot more for Travis than what she wanted to let on. Although, if he truly wanted Shanna, she would step back and allow it.

At least she'd try to.

"I guess I can understand why you'd be concerned. From what I've heard about Shanna, she is not exactly a good person. Or at least, she's not good to men."

"No. But I'm guessing that no one was holding a gun to Travis's head and telling him that he had to purchase her bucket, so I assume he did it because he wanted to."

"I don't know. I think hers went after everyone else's. In fact, I think he bought it after you left with Chalmer."

"Yeah. I'm pretty sure that's true. I didn't see it auctioned off at all anyway." She had remembered when she was walking out that Mr. Higginbotham had been saying that they had found a couple more buckets. Shanna's must have been one of those.

Not that it mattered. Although, she hadn't even considered that Travis might have been standing there when she had been bought and hadn't bought her himself.

They were just friends. Why would he buy her?

She tried to lift her chin up and push down all of the swirling feelings of pain and disappointment and not being good enough that wanted to rise to the surface. All those feelings that she felt in high school and thought that she had gotten over. Maybe she'd only gotten over them because she thought Travis and she had something going on together, something they would pick up when he came home.

She had waited for ten years. But she couldn't really blame Travis. They both changed a lot in those years. She didn't regret not pursuing any romantic relationships. She'd accomplished a lot more with her dogs and her cows than she would have if she had been tangled up with a man.

Still, she wanted a home and family of her own, and maybe she would already have had that if she hadn't been...waiting for Travis.

They made a couple of comments about the festival, and how well it was going, and how much money they probably made from all of the buckets that had been sold and the other items that had been donated for the auction, and then Claudia walked out beside her as she carried a tea towel that she wet at the sink along with the ice and another dry towel.

They parted at the door with Ellen going outside and Claudia saying that if she needed a nurse, come on back in and Claudia would get her sister, who was a registered RN.

Ellen said she would and then opened the door to walk outside.

Travis stood at the swing set, pushing one of the children on the swing, while Shanna stood beside him, her hands on her hips, her mouth going, but Ellen was unable to hear exactly what she was saying.

She stopped talking as Ellen got closer.

"Shouldn't you be sitting down?" she said to Travis, knowing that he had taken a couple rather bad blows to his head. If she had taken those blows, she knew that her head would be pounding with a headache at the very least.

"I guess I was waiting for you," he said easily, and he didn't look at Shanna as he left the swing and walked over, sitting down at the bench that was situated beside the swing set.

"Are you just going to leave him on the swing?" Shanna said, acting like she wasn't standing right there beside the swing.

"I think you can watch him while I put some ice on his jaw to help with this swelling and wipe off the blood." Ellen didn't realize that she could be so commanding and bossy as she listened to the words come out of her mouth.

They shut Shanna down, and she turned to the swing and took care of her child.

"Grr," Travis said, humor in his tone.

"You'd better just shut up and let me see your face, or I'll yell at you, too," she said, although her voice didn't hold any of the strident anger that she'd directed toward Shanna.

"Yes, ma'am," Travis said, and she felt like he was eighteen again, and they weren't adults, with adult problems and adult lives.

Like he hadn't just bought Shanna's lunch pail and committed to eating with her.

Of course, he had bought Ellen as well. She tried to remind herself of that, but he hadn't bothered to begin with. Only moved to keep her from being dragged away by Chalmer.

"I take it Chalmer disappeared?" she asked, lifting her head and looking around.

"Yeah. I hope that'll be the last of it. I should have called the police, but I didn't want him to drag you away any further than what he already had."

"I appreciate you taking care of me. I...didn't appear very grateful, I'm sure, and I really was. I didn't want to be with him."

"So are you thanking me for buying you? Or just for having a fistfight over you?"

She laughed. That wasn't exactly what happened. "Both," she said as she dabbed at the blood on his face.

"Ouch," he said, but the word didn't have any heat and not much emphasis either.

"I'm sorry. I guess I don't really need to get every single spot of dried blood off, but that's what you see them doing in the movies anyway."

He laughed. "I've never been confused about whether or not I belonged in the movies."

"Me either. I wouldn't want to be, although it's not like opportunities are dropping in my lap either."

"Can I say that I'm happy about that?"

Chapter Nine

Travis knew his serious tone took the conversation in a completely different direction. He felt a little bad about that since he always enjoyed their banter and the easy relationship they had. He should just be happy getting that back, but he couldn't seem to stop being serious.

He should have known she wouldn't let him.

"Why? So you don't have to start watching movies with your eyes closed?" She bumped her arm against his shoulder and then said, "Hold still, I don't think this is going to need stitches, but I'll know for sure once I get this dried blood."

"It's not bleeding; it won't need to be stitched."

"So I say hold still, and the man starts talking."

"I haven't seen you in five years. Of course I'm going to be talking."

"Just wait another five minutes, and then you could talk all night if you want to." She glanced over at the swing where Shanna's youngest child was throwing a fit because his brother was being pushed higher than he was. "Except, you probably ought to be paying some attention to your date."

One side of his lips pulled back, and he refrained from saying that he really didn't give a flip what happened to Shanna, he just wanted to be with Ellen, but that wasn't what he was supposed to do. He had bought her bucket, as much as he felt like he was forced into it, so that wasn't the way he should be. He should be a little more charming than what he had managed to be so far. He almost snorted at the idea. Getting into a fistfight was not exactly being charming.

Although, he did feel like the fistfight wasn't exactly his fault.

"You're right. You're always right." He didn't have to be happy about it though.

She didn't look very happy about it either. The laughter had drained from her eyes, and she had a look of concentration on her face. Rightfully so, since she was probing at the sore spot on his face, but he liked it better when her eyes shone with humor and happiness. That was the way he thought of Ellen. That, and how adorable she was with her cows and dogs.

"We're going to eat. I guess you guys can stand there all day and fiddle around with that if you want to." Shanna came over carrying one child that was crying on her hip as the other small child grabbed her legs.

"I have to pee!" the little guy said.

"You're wearing a diaper. Just pee in it," Shanna said, and the irritation in her voice was unmistakable.

"We're almost done. I just want to make sure he doesn't need stitches."

"He's not a baby," Shanna said. "And he bought my lunch. We're supposed to be eating together. Not sitting around while you fiddle with his face."

"I'm sorry," Ellen said, and Travis had to resist the urge to grab hold of her and tell her that she didn't have to apologize. He appreciated the fact that she was humble and that she hadn't bought into the world's idea of standing up for herself. Or whatever other such nonsense they talked about that wasn't biblical.

"We'll be over in a minute," Travis said, trying not to move his mouth as he spoke. Ellen wouldn't get angry at him, but it would make what she was doing harder.

"This has to hurt," she murmured.

"I'd do it again in a heartbeat. I like how things turned out." His words came out a little slurred as he spoke again without moving his mouth. He tried not to smile either, but his words made him want to. After all, they were true. He would much rather have Ellen here fussing over him than off with Chalmer somewhere. Regardless of the fact that he was trying to drag her despite her protests. That alone would make him happy that he'd stoop to the level of teenage boy again. A position he thought he'd outgrown years ago. Apparently, when it came to Ellen, he hadn't grown up at all.

"Well, I do too, but I guess I would rather be with Chalmer right now than have you sitting here in pain. Especially knowing that it is my fault. This is going to look terrible tomorrow."

"So you're saying tomorrow I'm not going to be handsome anymore?" He said that not being serious at all, but Ellen nodded, not even cracking a smile.

"This pretty face will be all marked up."

"Pretty was not what I was going for."

She smirked. "You know I think you're handsome. And this is just going to make you look a little rugged. So, ruggedly handsome. You can pull that off for the next week or so."

"She thinks I'm ruggedly handsome. I'll take it."

"Now, you probably better get over there and keep Shanna happy."

"You're coming too."

"I'm pretty sure Shanna doesn't want me. And I don't want to get between you two."

"There is no getting between us. We're not standing that close."

Her brows drew down, and her hand paused as she adjusted the ice on his cheekbone.

"You bought her lunch. You must be rather close." And then, almost as though the words were dragged out of her, she said, "You didn't bid on me at all."

His eyes widened. He hadn't thought that Ellen might for one second think that he wouldn't have bought her if he had been there when she was for sale.

He shifted, not caring if the ice fell off his face, and he took her hand in his, looking up at her. "You were already gone when I walked in. I didn't even know where you were. I got bombarded as soon as I walked in that I needed to buy something, and Shanna's bucket was the only one left. Trust me, if there was anyone else in town available for sale, I would have bid on them in a heartbeat. I don't exactly have great memories of Shanna."

Ellen pulled both of her lips between her front teeth, and he could see the hurt that had been in her heart on her face.

"Sorry. I didn't mean for you to think that for one second." He kind of liked the idea that it had bothered Ellen, but hated that he'd hurt her. Even though it had been unintentionally.

He tried for a smile. "Plus, I get here, and you're running around with Chalmer in the dark outside alone. What was I supposed to think?"

"That you hadn't gotten there in time to buy me?"

"I thought you were married." He almost told her how scared that had made him, but he thought that maybe they should get their friendship reestablished before he worked for more, as much as he wanted to.

"Please, give me a little more credit than that," Ellen said, giving him a ghost of a smile, and the last of the pain faded from her face, which had been his goal.

"I'm sorry. I should have given you more credit, but you thought I would actually buy Shanna's meal on purpose."

"You did!" she said, but there was a smile on her face.

"I mean without being forced into it."

"Well, let me get this stuff gathered up, and then we better go over and sit down with her. Although, I know she'd be happy if I went somewhere else."

"But I wouldn't be." He pursed his lips, ready to tease her. "And plus, I bought you, so I get tonight and five days this week for eight hours. You're at my beck and call."

"Oh boy. I was wondering when you were going to figure that out."

"Oh, trust me, I knew it when I paid the bill." He winked at her, or tried to anyway with the swelling that seemed to be around his eye. "You're an expensive girl, Ellen O'Reily."

"Nobody made you buy me. I could be really cheap."

"No. You're worth every penny and more." Then, to keep everything light, he said, "And I'm going to get every penny out of you this week. So be prepared to work hard."

He squeezed her hand, and she squeezed back, and there seemed to be something that passed between them at that time. He wasn't sure exactly what it was, but he hoped it was the start of something beautiful.

Chapter Ten

Ellen felt an unfamiliar stirring in her stomach. She didn't usually get nervous around Travis, but those were definitely butterflies in her stomach. Of course, she hadn't been around Travis for five years, so she really didn't know exactly how she felt around him normally.

She hoped this wasn't the new way. She didn't like it. But there was something new about Travis, well, a lot of new things. He had definitely matured, both in his personality and physically. Jan had said that his shoulders had broadened, and that wasn't the least of it. He had a man's face, and his eyes held knowledge and competence that matched his confident bearing.

He had been a teenager she admired and had turned into a man she could love.

She tried to shake that thought from her head. He hadn't hinted at feeling anything more than friendship with her. He'd been so insistent on it when they parted before that she was kind of scared to cross that line. For now, maybe she'd just wait and hope he did. Wait and enjoy the relief she felt that he hadn't bought Shanna's lunch because he wanted to.

That was the best thing she heard all night.

It made it difficult to keep the smile off her face.

"Keep an eye on Atlas. I have to go to the bathroom and change this diaper." Shanna spoke as she walked by, barely glancing at them as she strode toward the community center.

Obviously she was upset because Travis's attention wasn't completely on her. Ellen felt a little bad about that. She hadn't meant to take Travis away. Travis was spending his time where he wanted to, and that probably upset Shanna just as much as anything.

Ellen couldn't blame her; she would be disappointed if Travis was giving all of his attention to Shanna. But she hoped that she could be mature enough to step back and allow Travis to make the decision about who he wanted to be with without her getting angry and upset about it.

After all, getting angry and upset wasn't going to change his mind. It might make him be a little nicer to her, just because he felt bad, but she wouldn't want that either. Wouldn't want him to be afraid of her anger and change what he was doing just because he was afraid of it.

"Travis?" A woman's voice, unsure and a little shaky, made Ellen turn and look.

A brunette, a little younger than Ellen, holding a baby in her arms, stood off to the side, as though afraid to interrupt.

Ellen's eyes shot to Travis. Did he know this woman?

There was no recognition in his eyes as he spoke. "Are you looking for me?"

"Are you Travis Feagley?"

His brows scrunched forward a bit as he nodded his head. "Yes?"

The woman swallowed hard, the movement making the tattooed flowers around her throat seem to shake their leaves. Then she moved a little closer, and Ellen peeked at the bundle in her arms, snuggled down so only its face was showing, the delicate lashes resting against soft cheeks and the face totally relaxed in sleep. She was no judge of babies, but she'd been around her brother and sister enough to know that this baby was...very young. Maybe not even six weeks old.

"I was with your brother Roger."

The woman waited, seeming to want Travis to respond somehow to that. He jerked his head up.

"This is his kid."

Ellen blinked. She had no idea that Roger had a child. Nor even a girlfriend for that matter. He had been troubled as a teen, but Travis had never given up on him, constantly offering him a position, asking him to help, pushing him to do something constructive with the interests that he had.

Travis had spent a lot of time talking to her about Roger over the years, his concerns for his brother, his hopes and dreams that both of his brothers would work together with him, and Ellen had thought that Roger finally came around the last few years. In fact, he had been in Brazil with Travis and had stayed down when Travis left.

But, as Ellen counted back, it had only been eight months since Roger had gone down.

She assumed Travis was doing the same calculations in his head. And came to the conclusion that the baby very well could be Roger's.

"I didn't know he had a child." His voice was soft, gentle, as though he were deliberately keeping his emotions in check so as not to scare the woman in front of him who looked frightened as a church mouse.

"I can't keep it. You need to take it."

She held the baby tight for a moment, and then as though she needed to do it quickly, she shoved her arms out, pushing the baby at Travis's chest.

His arms came around it, almost automatically, and she dropped away, backing up.

"Don't tell nobody," she said.

"Don't leave. Tell me about...him? Her? What's the baby's name?"

Ellen stepped closer to Travis and put a hand on his back, just lightly pressed there to let him know she was beside him. She could feel the panic welling up inside of him, could see that he was on the verge of chasing the woman down as she turned around. She couldn't blame him. This was quite a shock. Especially considering that he just got back into the country.

"It's Alice. That's the baby's name. A girl." She nodded at the bag she threw at Travis's feet. Ellen had barely noticed, but when she saw it, she reached down and picked it up. "There's a note in there along with everything else. Don't tell nobody," she said again.

"Are you in some kind of trouble?" Ellen asked, since that didn't seem to occur to Travis yet. She had assumed when the woman first handed the baby over that she couldn't afford a baby and was giving it to Travis. It might not be a well-known fact that he was a multimillionaire, but it was generally accepted around town that since he rubbed shoulders with Ford Hansen, he probably had money. Or he at least had access to someone who did.

But now, she wondered if the woman wasn't having different issues. If someone wasn't chasing her, or if maybe she was expecting to be arrested.

"I guess you could say that. Just take good care of her, okay?" Up until that point, the woman had seemed rather stiff and unemotional about the child, but when she asked for them to take care of the baby, her eyes filled with tears, and she took a deep breath, seeming to push them away.

"Of course we will," Ellen said immediately, feeling compassion well up inside of her. What could this woman possibly be dealing with that would make her give up her beloved baby?

"Maybe we can help you?" she added, forming it into a question, because she knew that the woman had already made up her mind to give up her baby and move on.

"No. It's best this way. I can't really afford her anyway, though...I love her."

"I'll make sure she knows that."

Ellen stared at the woman, wondering if she'd seen her before. But the tattoo wrapped around her neck, plus the sleeve tattoos she had on both arms, the double ring in her nose, and the cartilage piercing in her ear, while they weren't exactly unique anymore, they still made her rather distinctive, and Ellen was pretty sure that if she'd seen her before, she would remember it.

She was too young to be someone she had graduated with or even someone she had known in school. Sweet Water High was a small school, with less than a thousand students from kindergarten to twelfth grade.

Ellen couldn't say that she knew every single kid in school, but she knew most of them. Although maybe this woman was younger than what she looked.

"Do you need money?" Travis's words startled her.

She'd been so intent on trying to figure out the woman she'd almost forgotten he stood beside her holding the baby.

She should have thought the woman might need money.

"No. I just need my baby—Roger's baby—to be safe."

"She will be," Travis said with as much sincerity as she'd ever heard him use before. In fact, if the situation didn't feel so serious, Ellen would tease him a bit about falling in love with the baby at first sight. It was obvious he was smitten and that the baby had roused every protective instinct he owned, as he cradled her carefully, bending over just a little as though he would shield her from anything.

It was heartwarming to see, made her chest feel warm and shimmery and something else she'd never felt before, but it stirred in her soul clear down to her toes, and while she'd always admired Travis, she felt something more. Something stronger as she looked at him holding the tiny baby.

She supposed women through the ages had looked at men in the same way. Something about seeing a man holding a baby, and not just holding it, but holding it like they would face death itself in order to protect it, stirred every feminine cell she had and brought them to attention.

"You can keep in touch."

"I can't. I have to go."

They watched as she turned and hurried off, disappearing into the darkness.

"She doesn't even have a car," Ellen murmured.

"Maybe she just parked it a little ways away so we wouldn't see it and couldn't report her."

"Is it illegal to give someone a baby?" Ellen asked, thinking that it probably should be, although maybe not. Maybe it was better to do what this woman had done, to give her baby to someone she thought could take care of her, rather than abandon her completely. Or, worse yet, keep her but allow her to be abused.

No, Ellen had no doubt the woman loved the baby and thought she was doing the very best thing she could for her.

"I need to call Roger," Travis murmured.

"Are you two still standing there?" Shanna said, walking out with her baby held loosely on one hip.

Ellen had completely forgotten about Shanna. Although it wouldn't have surprised her, as angry as she seemed, if she would have walked back in and not come out again.

Travis would be honor bound to go in and get her, Ellen was sure, since he had bought her lunch bucket.

"You need to excuse me for a moment. I have a phone call to make," Travis said, barely looking at Shanna as he moved away.

Ellen almost offered to hold the baby, but it didn't look to her like Travis had any intention of giving her up. It was adorable, and she figured she could spend a lot of time just staring at him holding the little one, but he would probably appreciate her trying to appease Shanna more than her staring at him at the moment.

"Can I give you a hand with the kids and help get the food out on the table while he talks on the phone?"

"We're going to eat whether he does or not," Shanna snapped, grabbing the bucket from one end of the table, setting it down at the other, putting a child on the bench, and holding the other as she put first one leg and then the other over the side of the seat and sat down.

"You want me to go inside to get you drinks?" Ellen asked.

Shanna jerked her head up. "Shoot. I totally forgot about drinks."

"What would you guys like? I'll go and grab some. I don't think Travis will be long on the phone."

"He better not be. I want my money back. If I had known that he was going to completely ignore me, I wouldn't have been so interested in having him buy my meal."

Shanna had never been overly kind to her, but Ellen felt bad for her anyway. She could commiserate with that, even if she didn't blame Travis for not really wanting to spend a lot of time with her, not that he had much choice, since the night had been rather eventful. But it would hurt Shanna's feelings.

Knowing she was a poor substitute for Travis and Shanna didn't want her anyway, she hurried into the community building to grab some drinks.

Chapter Eleven

"Hey, Travis." Roger's voice was casual and easy on the other end of the line. Travis knew the time zones as well as someone who had lived in Brazil would, and he also knew that they were heading into fall, or the rainy season where Roger was. "You've only been gone a week. Surely you're not thinking that you need to check up on me already?"

He was feeling jet lagged. The traveling was exhausting, and he'd made it worse by pushing as hard as he could to get home to Ellen. He had really wanted to buy her bucket and catch up with her. Tonight had not gone as planned. That was for sure, he thought as he looked down at the little baby snuggled in his arms. For now, it was fine, since the baby seemed to be sleeping, but what was he going to do when she woke up? He had no clue how to take care of a baby.

Not to mention, how was he going to work and take care of an infant at the same time?

Surely he would be able to figure out some answers to his questions, but the first thing he needed to do was deal with his brother.

"You didn't tell me you had a baby," he said.

There was silence on the phone.

"Maybe that's because I didn't know I did," Roger said, enunciating each word clearly. Speaking slowly as though he were thinking.

It irritated Travis that he might have to try to figure out who he'd been sleeping with who could possibly be pregnant. He knew that that was the way the world worked, but he'd hoped that his brothers would be different. Maybe his expectations were too high. Not everybody did what he did, fell in love when he was a teenager, figured out exactly who he wanted, and then never even looked at anyone else.

Yeah, faithfulness wasn't exactly something that the world valued anymore. It definitely wasn't something that was on display in too many lives. He couldn't get mad at his brother just because he didn't have the virtue that Travis thought he should.

"I'm holding your baby right now," Travis said.

"Travis. I know that I don't have the best reputation, and I honestly had to think back, but it's been years. And that's no joke."

"That's funny. Since we're not elephants."

He didn't mean that in a funny way, but Roger laughed a bit anyway.

"Travis. I promise you. If I had a baby, I wouldn't be lying about it. And I probably wouldn't be content to be in Brazil. I know my reputation wasn't that great, maybe it still isn't, but you can't deny that over the last few years, I've been trying hard to change." Roger's voice held a pleading note that Travis tried to ignore. He didn't want to let his brother off the hook from his responsibilities.

Although, as he thought about it, Roger had a lot of faults, but lying hadn't been one of them. He'd been very straightforward about not wanting to do what was right. And he never minded that Travis knew that.

Had he started lying? Travis knew that sometimes people would do a lot of twisting around to save their reputation, to make people think better of them than what they were, to hide inconvenient truths. Like a baby.

"If it were possible for me to have a baby, I would tell you. What does the woman look like?"

She was pretty distinctive.

"You tell me."

Roger blew out a breath. It wasn't hard to hear his frustration through the telephone, even though he didn't say anything. Then finally, he said, "You know I have a weakness for blondes. In fact, I don't think I've ever had a girlfriend who wasn't a blonde. But I promise you, I can't say I'm lily white, that I've never committed fornication, but it's been years. That's the truth."

Travis looked down at the baby. Could the woman have been lying? Roger sounded so sincere. He had no reason to lie. Did he? Other than maybe not wanting to come home. Maybe he was afraid Travis would insist.

"I'll take care of it. I'm not telling you that you need to come back to the states."

"If I thought for one second it was my baby, I'd be begging you to let me come back."

Trying to think back on the girlfriends that Roger had brought home, Travis was sure he hadn't seen the mom, and he was sure there had been quite a few. For a long time, Travis thought Roger was going to go the way of their parents. Promiscuous, helped along with lots of drugs and alcohol. Unable to keep a job and uncaring about the people around them.

Thankfully, Roger had found the Lord. Travis always thought that mostly was thanks to Ellen, but he wasn't sure. Maybe there was someone else. But he didn't really question the why or the how, he just saw the results. Roger's life had changed. That had been about two and a half or three years ago.

"What did she say her name was?"

"The girl or the baby?" Travis asked before he realized that he didn't know the girl's name.

"The girl. I have no clue about the baby."

Roger's tone was dismissive. And it made it feel like Travis was being ridiculous for even asking. Like it was a given that he wouldn't know the baby's name. The fact that Roger didn't have a clue about that was absolutely clear.

"She didn't tell me her name. She had double piercings in her nose, a couple rings in the tops of her ears, and a bunch of tattoos. Solid tattoos on her arms."

"I never really cared for girls with tattoos." Roger let out a humorless laugh. "Not that there wasn't a time when I wasn't picky."

"Yeah."

Travis didn't say anything else. He wasn't going to rub Roger's past in his face, but he couldn't pretend that it didn't exist either. It was part of him, just like every person's past was a part of them. God forgave the sin, He promised to remember it no more, but that didn't mean that the consequences weren't there. Consequences sometimes lasted a lifetime.

"Travis. Just tell me. If you want me to come home, I will. If you want me to take a paternity test, I'll gladly do that too. I'm telling you, the kid isn't mine. But if it needs someone to take care of them, I can come home and do it if that's what you're going to insist on."

"I'm not going to insist you take care of a child that's not yours. I just... I didn't think to question the woman when she said it was."

"I know I should get mad about that, but I understand. I feel like I've changed. Like I've proven that I have. I'm nothing like the man I used to be, but I get that it might be harder for you to understand or see."

"No. I believe in you. I know you've changed, not because of you, but because of Jesus."

"Amen."

"When she came up to me, I didn't think about all of that, and I just believed it, because that's kind of what I was conditioned to do for a long time."

"Because of me. I can't expect you to totally forget what I used to be. Even if I feel like it's completely passed."

"All right. So you're sure this baby isn't yours?"

"I'm sure."

Now what?

"What are you gonna do?" Roger asked, and although the situation was serious, and their conversation had not been less so, there was humor in Roger's voice, as though he were just now realizing that Travis was in quite a predicament. Since he didn't know the name of the mother and he was holding a baby that someone was going to have to take care of.

"I'm not sure. I...never had this kind of situation dropped in my lap before."

"You're the only person I know who would call a baby a situation."

"Well, it is."

"So is there anything else you wanted? Or were you just going to make me assume my parental responsibilities, mistakenly."

"No, that was it. And you don't have to rub it in."

"I guess I think it's kind of funny. Maybe next time, you have a little more faith in me before you just take a baby from any woman who wants to give you one."

"Shut up, bro." Travis rolled his eyes. He was going to be hearing about this for a long time. "See if you can get that paternity test figured out."

"Now you shut up."

"You want me to believe you. Prove it." Travis was ninety-nine percent sure that Roger wasn't the father, but if Roger was going to give him a hard time, he could push the paternity test. Just to push back on Roger. Although, when it came up that Roger wasn't the father, Roger would never let him live it down.

"So how do you go about getting a paternity test?"

"I've had no reason to ever research the question. In any way."

"There is a very small circle of people where you can actually say that and it sounds like bragging."

"The circle might be bigger than you think it is. And it's got the most important Being in the world in it, so yeah. Call it bragging if you want."

Roger laughed without humor, knowing that Travis was rubbing it in just a bit.

"All right. I'll call you some other time when I'm not panicking."

"My big brother, panicking. You know, this sounds like a job for Ellen." Roger laughed and then slid his phone off, leaving Travis standing with a dead phone to his ear.

Actually, Roger might be onto something. This did sound like a good job for Ellen.

Chapter Twelve

W hen Travis came back to the table, he was serious and quiet, the baby still tucked in his arm and thankfully still sleeping. Ellen wasn't sure he knew what to do with a crying baby, and she was pretty sure that Travis wasn't going to want to learn in front of Shanna.

Both of Shanna's kids were fussy and tired, and Shanna didn't have a whole lot of patience with them.

Ellen felt bad for the children and did as much as she could to help, but knew the three of them all needed a good night's sleep.

Finally, Shanna packed up and said she was leaving, but instead of heading to her car, she walked toward the community center, like she didn't want to leave the fellowship of the town.

Ellen felt a little bad for her. She was an extrovert, who needed interaction with people in order to charge her batteries, and it must be very hard to have to even spend one day at home alone with two small children. Shanna worked outside the home, she had since before the divorce, and so she got to see people on a regular basis, but Ellen figured that two little kids weren't exactly her idea of ideal company.

Of course, Ellen had been sitting at the picnic table with her, so obviously Ellen wasn't Shanna's idea of ideal company either.

But Ellen tried not to think about that too hard. After all, she wasn't exactly anyone's ideal company.

"Roger says it isn't his," Travis finally said after they'd sat in silence for a while, him staring down at the baby, as though he were thinking hard.

No wonder he was thinking hard.

"Roger denied it?" Ellen asked, unbelieving.

"He pointed out that he changed. I know he has, but when she said that it was his, it was easy to believe, because of his past reputation."

"Yeah. I guess he has changed. He... He really isn't the kind of person to have a baby he didn't know about anymore. I...feel a little bad that I was so willing to believe the worst of him immediately." She paused, not wanting to say something insulting. "Did he say that there really wasn't any possible way?"

How else did she ask if he had sex with anyone before he left the country? It was a little awkward, but that was really what she was trying to get out.

"Yeah. He said it had been years. Probably since he truly started to live for the Lord."

"Wow. Okay. So... It's not like we can just give the baby back."

"No. I'm just sitting here thinking I have no idea how to handle a baby. What to do, how to take care of her, anything."

"I have a little bit more experience, because of my brother and sister, but it's a big responsibility. And I know there were multiple times I was happy that it was not me in charge. Particularly when they were sick. But when they were that age, they were up a lot at night."

"Yeah. I don't know how I can take care of a baby and continue to work. Although... I really didn't come back here to continue my business things, I have a few loose ends to wrap up, but I had planned to buy a ranch."

He'd talked about his plans with her, so that wasn't a shock, but the baby was going to throw a wrench into everything.

"Do you think she might have gotten Roger and Edgar mixed up?" She hated to ask about Travis's other brother. The woman had had another man's baby. Surely she knew the name of that man.

"I didn't ask. But...it's not like they look a lot alike, and Edgar, while he's had his moments, wasn't like Roger."

Ellen nodded and didn't say anything else. Edgar hadn't been involved with drugs or alcohol, and while he'd had a couple of girlfriends, he wasn't known as being promiscuous.

"She said she left some instructions in the bag," Ellen remembered suddenly, reaching under the picnic table where she'd moved the bag so it was out of the way.

"I'd forgotten. Totally forgotten about the bag. I don't even know what to do, but I know I'll need a car seat at least. It's too late to get one tonight, plus, I can hardly drive to the store with no car seat. What would I do, hold her in my lap?"

"I can text Claudia. She's in charge of the missionary closet at church. I'm sure there's a car seat in there we can use."

Ellen had already pulled her phone out and sent a quick text off to Claudia. The missionary closet held all kinds of donations the people from the church had either bought and donated or donated after they were done with them, things their children had outgrown, clothing for the most part, but there were always car seats and high chairs and that type of thing. Often missionaries didn't take those things, because most people already had a car seat and also a lot of those items were too bulky for them to haul around the country while they were on deputation.

So they had a tendency to languish in the closet. Which was actually a rather large storage room. Not a closet.

"You can tell her I'll return it soon as I'm able to get one for myself."

"This is what it's for. People in need. This baby isn't yours."

"It might be best for everyone involved if I say that she is." He took a breath, then continued, "I feel like she is. She was given to me. That makes her mine. Right?"

Ellen froze, looking up at him. She hadn't considered that. She didn't know what she was thinking, but when she heard that the baby wasn't Roger's, she assumed that...Travis wouldn't be keeping her. She had actually thought Travis wouldn't keep her any longer than it would take to get Roger here and get him to claim ownership of the baby.

It sounded like Travis was thinking about keeping her forever.

She supposed that was the right thing to do.

"Are you afraid that woman was actually in trouble? Is that why you're saying it's best for everyone to think that it's just yours?"

"Yeah. She seemed scared. And if she claimed that it was Roger's, and Roger says there's no way that it could be his, she lied. I guess because of the way she seemed petrified, not even giving us her name, and leaving immediately, even though I thought it was obvious that she loved the baby, I just thought that rather than needing money, like I thought first, that she was afraid for its life for some reason."

"Yeah. I thought at first she wanted money too, but if that were true, surely she would just say it was your brother's baby and you need to give her a certain amount. She could have said one million dollars, and that wouldn't have been out of the realm of possibility."

"Exactly. She could ask for a lot of money. Enough to set her up for life. But she didn't ask for a cent."

"No. That's a good point." Ellen felt a chill go down her backbone. What could possibly make this woman so afraid that she would give up her baby in order to protect her?

She knew that drugs could do scary things to people. And there was a whole world out there that she really didn't know anything about. She'd never been involved in drugs in any way, thankfully. Her world had revolved around cattle and dogs and the farm, and none of that was particularly scary, although it was dangerous at times.

But dangerous in a straightforward way. Not dangerous in a drug lord out to get you for some addiction that you can't control kind of way.

To her mind anyway, it was a much bigger danger.

"I'm a little scared. To be honest. I've heard really terrible things about drug lords and what those people will do in order to get money."

"Yeah. It can be pretty nasty."

She didn't ask how Travis knew, but she assumed that in South America he'd seen more than a little bit of that.

She started digging through the bag, trying to put drugs and killers and thugs who might be lurking around any dark corner out of her mind. If she started thinking about that, she'd be afraid to take one step in the dark.

"Here's a piece of paper," she said, pulling it out and turning it toward the streetlight so she could see the writing on it. "It looks like instructions."

"Good. Hopefully they're very detailed." He paused. "It makes me a little nervous that she was able to fit all the instructions for the care of a human child on one sheet of paper."

"One side of one sheet of paper," Ellen corrected him after she flipped the paper over and saw there was no writing on the back.

"Is there a phone number I can call?"

She skimmed down the page. "No. No phone number. No email address, and...no name."

"Man. I know you're probably right to be afraid about the whole drug thugs, but...this scares me worse."

"The responsibility of having a human life all on your shoulders?" Ellen said, understanding how chilling it could feel to be the one responsible for keeping the small one alive.

"Yeah. That's exactly right."

"Well, the instructions are about how much she eats, when to feed her, and her favorite songs."

"That's it?"

Ellen skimmed over the paper again. "Yes. That's it."

"All right. That doesn't leave me with much."

She fingered through the bag. "There are diapers. Not a lot, and a baby goes through a lot. I would say there are enough diapers for two or maybe three days."

"All right. I can make it to the store in the next two or three days, if I have a car seat."

As he spoke, her phone buzzed.

She picked it up and read the text.

> Sure. The closet isn't locked, so go help yourself.

She barely had finished reading a text when another one came in.

> Not to be nosy, but are you pregnant?

She laughed a little, and Travis said, "What's so funny?"

"Claudia wants to know if I'm pregnant."

"No. That's me."

They laughed together. Knowing that in some circles, that idea might not be quite as funny as it was to them.

"All right. Thanks a lot for talking me through this. I thought that the time that I spent away had helped me become a more confident person able to handle whatever life throws at them. I was not expecting life to throw me a baby."

"I think that was the Lord who tossed you this child, and I don't think it was an accident," Ellen said.

Now that she had a little time to process, she could remember that everything that happened to a person in their life came through the Lord. Obviously, this was just one more thing that God had given, and he picked the perfect man to do it. She couldn't imagine a better father than Travis.

"She's going to need a mom," Travis murmured softly. "Or I'm going to need a nanny, at least."

She held her breath. Then she thought she was being silly. If he wanted her to be the mom or the nanny, he would ask her. He wouldn't just throw a sentence like that out there.

"Well, you hired me for the week. I can help you with that, along with everything else. I can get the car seat, I can even make a diaper run, and I assume you're going to run out of formula, too, although it says she only eats four ounces at a time right now."

"I suppose that's four ounces every two hours?"

"Ashley fed her babies every two to three hours, but she nursed them. I've always heard that bottle-fed babies can go a little longer. But I suppose it depends on the baby. Right now, she's pretty soundly asleep."

"I keep touching her to make sure she's breathing. It looks like she's sleeping, but when she's not moving like that, she could be dead."

"I remember Tadgh and Ashley getting up in the middle of the night and sometimes during the day just to go over and stand by the crib and make sure their baby was breathing. I think that's a natural human instinct any time you're around a baby and you have any ounce of compassion at all."

"Well, that's a relief. I have compassion. And more than an ounce. It wasn't exactly something I had been dying to find out today, but it's still news."

She laughed and then realized she'd never answered Claudia.

No. I'm seriously asking for a friend.

"Are you really going to let everyone think this is your baby?" she asked, knowing that that was probably the best way, especially if the mother needed to be protected, but knowing that it wasn't really fair to Travis, considering that it wasn't true, and it would change the way people thought about him.

"I think that's best." He didn't sound overly happy about it, but he did sound determined. His voice matched the jutting out of his chin and the way he nodded his head decisively.

Her phone buzzed.

What friend?

"If you're going to tell anyone, Claudia wants to know what friend I'm asking about the missionary closet for."

"I guess now is as good a time as any. Although, people might remember that when I walked in, I wasn't holding anything. They might wonder where the baby was then, and there will be some awkward questions. Do you think you can put it off until tomorrow?"

They were just winging it, and she didn't blame him for not wanting to face any questions this evening.

"Yeah. Definitely. I'll just tell her I'll talk to her about it tomorrow. I have to get up early and do the aquatics instruction at the Olympic training center, but after that, I can help you all day and meet with Claudia too."

"All right. I guess that means I'm on my own for tonight."

She bit her lip. She would like to help him. But if he was going to do this, claim the baby as his own, she wasn't sure what kind of rumors would swirl around both of them if she was there beside him. Everyone knew she wasn't pregnant, but they just came out of a long, brutal winter. She could have worn bulky clothes and hidden the pregnancy. It had been done before.

"Yeah. I guess you are."

"Stop that," he said, indicating where she had her lip between her teeth. "I wasn't trying to pressure you into anything. Nothing more than helping me find someone who can be a mother...wife."

He said that a little oddly, but she couldn't figure out exactly what he was trying to say, so she nodded. "Yes. I will be there tomorrow, after I'm done teaching aquatics, and I'll help you with whatever you need. Getting diapers and formula for the baby, finding a wife. Easy-peasy."

She hated the way her stomach boiled and twisted. It wasn't quite the same as seeing him with Shanna. Shanna was a different feeling entirely. Mostly because Shanna had used him in high school and didn't care about anyone but herself.

That's what she told herself, anyway. Mostly she just wished that she could take the offer back. But she could hardly do that since she was stuck with him for the week, because he saved her from Chalmer and bought her himself.

She wanted to shake her head and complain about small towns and their idiosyncrasies, the crazy things they did in order to earn money to put in parks and fix up sidewalks.

At least her labor was going to a good cause. Sweet Water was very frugal, and the money would be put to good use. Now she just had to serve her time with a good attitude.

She never thought she'd have to try to force herself to want to be in Travis's company, but the idea of finding a wife for him, one who wasn't her, anyway, while she had to spend the entire week with him was almost enough to make her beg off.

But she wasn't in the habit of not keeping her word. And she didn't want that to become something that was easy for her. Doing it even one time just felt like a slippery slope.

She typed back a reply to Claudia, letting her know that she would meet her tomorrow and talk to her about it then.

Claudia was fine with it and sent back an

Okay, looking forward to it.

"I guess I should head to the church and see what I can find for you."

"Yeah, if you don't mind."

"Are you going to come along?"

"I'm a little afraid to be alone right now. I feel very needy," he said with a short laugh.

"All right. Come on. We'll get you a car seat. We can handle this. People have been raising humans since God created Adam and Eve. If they can do it, we can do it, too."

She realized that she said "we," instead of "you," but she didn't correct herself. For now, it was her helping him. He didn't want her to be anything more than a friend, and she wasn't going to throw a big fit about it. She had decided when she was a teenager that she was going to be the very best friend to him that she could be, and nothing was going to change in that area. Friends didn't drop each other just because one of them did something the other didn't like or that hurt their feelings. She didn't want to be that kind of friend anyway. That wasn't her best.

And it wasn't the kind of friend Travis deserved. He deserved a friend who stuck by him no matter what. Of course, once he had a wife, she'd need to back away. After all, a wife wasn't going to want Travis to have another woman as his best friend. No way. But until then, Ellen could help him in every way she could. That is what a good friend did.

Chapter Thirteen

Travis stared down at the bundle in his arms, standing in the darkened living room of the house that he'd grown up in. Roger was in Brazil, and Edgar was off on an assignment for Ford Hansen. Ford had taken all three brothers under his wing, and Travis owed him more than he could say or ever repay. But right now, that wasn't the thought on his mind.

Instead, first and foremost, was keeping this baby alive through the night. The second thing was trying to figure out how to convince Ellen that she should be his wife.

When he suggested that she help him find a wife, he had been joking and had intended to say that she would be perfect. Hint, hint.

After all, he wasn't going to find someone who would marry him this week, as much as he needed help with the baby. And he wouldn't want to marry someone just to get them to do the job of a nanny. That wasn't right or fair.

But he hadn't been able to get the words out before she'd taken what he said seriously and jumped into it the way Ellen always did, with both feet and her whole heart. She would do everything in her power to find him a perfect wife.

He suspected she'd be asking Claudia tomorrow whenever she met with her, and she'd be talking to all the ladies at her aquatics class about it first thing in the morning as well.

What a mess. Not that he thought that there were going to be a million women knocking down his door tomorrow, but he didn't want to have even one. He wanted Ellen. Only his stupid tongue and his overburdened brain couldn't seem to get together.

He could call her right now and fix it, but the baby was starting to stir, and that set fire to the tiny bit of panic that had been nestling in his chest all evening.

He could do this.

Lord, I know everything happens for a reason. And You don't give us anything that You're not going to help us handle, but I'm a little scared right now. Please help me not to kill this baby.

He knew that he was scraping the bottom of the barrel. He should have his sights set a lot higher. He should be praying for grace and strength to raise the child up in the nurture and the admonition of the Lord. Right now, he had one goal, and that was a live baby come morning.

"All right. I'm going to have to set you down, because I can't make a bottle with just one hand. Maybe when I get better at this." He spoke softly, knowing that before when he and Ellen had been talking, the baby seemed to be calmed by their voices, but this made her little eyes blink as she seemed to pull herself from sleep, and the next thing he knew, her face scrunched up and turned beet red, and the loudest noise he'd ever heard from another human came out of that little tiny, rosebud mouth.

This was his problem to deal with.

He looked around to see if there was anyone standing nearby that he could hand her off to.

But he was still in his deserted living room, the only person in the house.

Ellen hadn't even come in. She set the car seat down by the door and seemed reluctant to leave, but she didn't ask to stay, and he didn't ask her to.

Things were going to be dicey enough, come morning when the whole town wanted to know where in the world the mother for this baby was. They didn't need the rumors swirling around them tonight. He appreciated her discretion on the matter, even while he wished she didn't have it, and that she was here beside him now.

He got his phone, and with one thumb, while the baby continued to cry, he texted her.

> She's crying.

> Is she hungry?

Ellen's answer came back immediately like she had been sitting by the phone waiting to see if he needed help. Which would be quintessential Ellen. She had always been there for him anytime he needed her. But there had been long stretches of time when they hadn't talked at all, and he felt like that was Ellen giving him room to grow and change.

> I don't know. I don't know how to make a bottle.

> Are you still holding her?

> Yes

> Put her down.

> But she's crying!

> She's crying, not dying. Put her down so you can make a bottle.

His phone beeped as he walked into the kitchen, and he set the baby gently down on the counter. Was it safe to put a baby down on the counter?

> Get the formula out of the baby bag. There are instructions on the side of the can.

He took a breath. He could do this.

> Don't leave me.

> I'm right here. You can call me if you need me.

> I won't be able to hear you because the baby is crying too loud. She's tiny, but she makes the loudest noise I've ever heard a human make.

Ellen sent a laughing emoji in reply.

He rolled his eyes, glad Ellen thought it was funny. Actually, she was right, it was a little bit funny. But he wouldn't be able to laugh until the baby wasn't crying anymore.

Fumbling with the formula can, he read the instructions: two ounces of water, one scoop of formula. He assumed that meant that he put the water in first.

> You can use warm water. But not too hot.

He glanced at his phone and read her text without touching it. Ellen would understand that he needed both hands to make the formula. He'd thank her later.

Putting warm water up to the 4-ounce line, he took the lid off the formula, saw that the can was almost empty, and sighed. He was able to get two scoops out and stick the lid back on the bottle. While he shook it with one hand, he texted with the other.

> She only sent one can, and I don't think there's even enough formula to last the night.

> I'll go get some.

> No. You have to work in the morning. Plus, it's at least an hour drive to Rockerton then back.

That was where the closest store was that might be open at this time of night.

I'll be there in an hour and a half, tops.

He shook his head, smiling. Relieved. He didn't want her to be put out, but at the same time, he didn't want to end up here with no formula and a crying baby. Although, he had a car seat now, so he could conceivably take the baby to the store, except it felt like a little much, to have the baby in the store, especially if she was crying, trying to figure out what formula to get.

Send me a picture of the formula can so I get the right stuff.

He took a picture, sent it, and then picked up the baby.

He couldn't remember any of the songs that the note had said the baby liked, except for one. He started to sing it.

Blessed assurance, Jesus is mine!
Oh, what a foretaste of glory divine!
Heir of salvation, purchase of God,
Born of His Spirit, washed in His blood.

To his surprise, even before the bottle touched her lips, the baby stopped crying and her big, dark eyes, so blue they almost looked black, looked up at him, blinking.

Nice. But the moment he stopped singing, her face scrunched up again, prompting him to start again immediately. If it would keep her from crying, he would sing all night.

This is my story, this is my song,
Praising my Savior all the day long;
This is my story, this is my song,
Praising my Savior all the day long.

He managed to get the bottle in her mouth. She had been

mesmerized looking at his face, listening to his voice, maybe even feeling the vibrations of his chest, but after a second or two, she realized what was in her mouth. She shook a little, and then her mouth closed around the nipple and she started sucking greedily. He kept singing just because she liked it, and he did too. He swayed a little as he sang.

Perfect submission, perfect delight,
Visions of rapture now burst on my sight;
Angels, descending, bring from above
Echoes of mercy, whispers of love.
Perfect submission, all is at rest,
I in my Savior am happy and blest,
Watching and waiting, looking above,
Filled with His goodness, lost in His love.

This is my story, this is my song,
Praising my Savior all the day long;
This is my story, this is my song,
Praising my Savior all the day long.

He didn't know whether he'd sung the song fifty or a hundred times before he heard a car in the driveway.

By that time, he'd gone in the living room and sat down on the recliner. He hadn't put his feet up but had kept them on the floor, rocking back and forth. Alice stopped sucking the bottle when there was still half an ounce or so left, and checking the instructions, he realized he was supposed to burp her. He searched that on the Internet and watched a video, never stopping his song.

When she burped, she spit formula all over his shoulder. He hadn't thought to have any kind of rag on it, but after watching the video, he'd realized spitting was kind of normal. He wasn't sure exactly how much was normal, but a couple of the babies that he'd seen on the video had spit up whenever they burped as well.

That made sense to him, but it was one of the questions he wanted to ask Ellen when she came—how much spit-up was normal.

She knocked softly on the door but didn't wait for him to call out before she stepped in the house.

Any time he saw Ellen, he felt drawn to look at her, but tonight more than ever. She was like a balm for his soul. She carried two large bags, and Chewy was at her heels.

"Is Chewy okay?"

He nodded. There hadn't been too many times growing up that Ellen had come to his house. Most of the time, it was him going to hers. But they spent a few different times in the kitchen, cooking for his brothers when one of them was sick, and she'd been over a couple times to care for him when he'd been down with the flu or some other illness.

There was no reason for Chewy to be in the house, and she'd never come in with her.

"She's asleep?" She nodded at the baby.

"She really likes 'Blessed Assurance.'"

"That's what the instructions said."

It seemed like an odd song for a baby to like, but maybe that was why it stuck in his head. "I couldn't remember any of the other ones." He felt bad for not getting up. "I'm afraid to move."

She told Chewy to lie down on the rug by the door, then she moved through the dining room and into the living room, holding up the two bags.

"I got four containers of formula and four packages of diapers. This is just half of it. I wasn't sure how long a can of formula would last, but I figured four cans would at least get you through the night."

He laughed a little. It would more than get them through the night. And he appreciated her making sure that he had plenty. Now he didn't have to worry about going to the store anytime soon.

"Man. That stuff is expensive." She peered over his shoulder and smiled at the sleeping baby. "If you don't mind, I'm just going to set it on your table here, run out, and get the other bags. And then, it looks like you're good."

She started walking toward the table, and then she froze. "Oh! I wasn't sure exactly how old Alice is, and whether or not she is rolling, so I got a pack and play for you. It will work as a crib if you want it to, and that will give you a place to keep the baby so you don't have to worry about her rolling off anywhere, just in case she's at that stage."

"I set her on the counter."

Ellen's eyes got big, and her brows went way up. "She didn't roll off?"

"No. But she was crying so hard she moved herself around a little bit."

"Did you change her diaper?"

"I've never changed a diaper in my life before. I'm going to have to YouTube that too."

"YouTube that...too? So you YouTubed something else?"

"Burping."

"I see. Well, she must have burped. That's what that big wet spot is on your shoulder."

"Yeah. It's kinda sticky. Is that normal?"

"Spitting up when she burps? Yes."

"The amount."

"I'm...not sure. It can seem like a lot, but I think it's probably okay."

"Hmm." He would have to take her word for it.

"I know I shouldn't stay. But if you want me to hold her while you change and set the pack and play up, I can." Ellen lifted her brows.

"I really hate to ask you. You've already done more for me than a normal person should have to, and I feel like I'm really taking advantage of our friendship."

"No. That's what friends are for." She held her hands out for the baby, and he handed her over gently. She stirred a little but didn't wake. She'd been snuggled down nice and warm, and settled back as Ellen gently bounced her and swayed at the same time.

"You look like you've done that a time or two."

"Having younger siblings is a real benefit at times." Ellen laughed. "I didn't always appreciate them."

"Seems to me like when I came to visit you when your siblings were babies, you should have put me to work, instead of allowing me to just watch."

"I didn't know it was going to come down to this." Ellen laughed.

And he loved the sound. It stirred something deep in his soul. But it didn't seem like the right time to talk about that.

"This is quite a welcome present for you. You're gone for five years and come home to this."

"Yeah. It was not what I was expecting, but I've had a lot of things in life that weren't quite what I was expecting." Coming home and hearing Chalmer talk about owning Ellen had been far worse than having a baby thrust at him.

He walked out and got the pack and play and the other bags of groceries, carrying everything in. He had spent a lot of late nights working on business-related things, getting reports ready, making PowerPoint presentations for a board meeting, and a myriad of other things, but this was the first time that he'd been up this late with Ellen, other than the one time they'd delivered the puppies so long ago.

She was tired. Her eyes were red rimmed, and her eyelids drooping, but she wasn't grumpy. He appreciated that. He'd seen too many men who were stuck in a lifetime relationship with women who were either perpetually grumpy, easy to set off, or never satisfied. Ellen wasn't any of those things.

Of course, if he looked for a woman of character, someone who tried to live what she believed, he wouldn't have to worry about getting someone who was any of those things, but Ellen just lived it all so beautifully that he didn't have to think about it, he just compared other women to her and found them wanting.

He thought about Shanna and the way she had acted with her children earlier in the evening. She'd been irritated and short and unkind. She'd taken her irritation out on them, and him, and, he was sure, on Ellen too.

But he hadn't seen Ellen be anything but kind.

A person didn't just naturally become that way, they had to work hard at it, to become something that wasn't natural. Ellen had, and it was obvious that Shanna had not.

He wondered if maybe it was because everything had always come easy to Shanna. And then, when life started to get a little hard, she wasn't prepared for that, because she'd never been tested before.

He supposed his rough childhood, and the fact that Ellen had lost her mom when she was little and had been raised by her uncle, never really fitting in with her friends at school, had been what had prompted them to be able to meet challenges with a bit of grace.

That, and he couldn't discount the influence Jesus had on their lives.

Shanna would claim to be a Christian. So there was that. There had to be a deliberate desire to do what God wanted, he supposed.

He hadn't figured it out by the time he got the pack and play together and turned to Ellen, who was still holding and bouncing the baby.

"Just in time. She's starting to stir."

He glanced at the clock. "I suppose it's about time for her to have another bottle."

"It would probably be a good time to change her diaper too."

"Oh boy. Can you hold her for just a little bit more while I find a video online?"

"Or I could show you how to do it?" Ellen lowered her head and looked at him, and he grinned sheepishly.

"Do you mind?"

"Not at all."

He knew she wouldn't, he just...hadn't thought about asking her and felt a little foolish for needing to. But he didn't want to do it wrong. Surely there was a wrong way. Although, as he thought back at some of the people who had been able to raise children to adulthood, his mom included in that group, he figured that it couldn't possibly be rocket science, otherwise there would be a lot more dead babies in the world.

The thought was sobering, rather than humorous.

"When they're really young, they can't roll. But you never know when they're going to be able to, so you can't ever set them down without making sure that they're on a surface they can't roll off of."

He nodded his head.

"I remember Ashley telling me that. I think it was something they told her in the hospital. Every once in a while, she would set the baby in the middle of the bed and maybe run to the bathroom or something, but you just have to be careful."

"Once you drop it, you can't put it back together."

"I suppose that's one way of looking at it," she said, giving him a glance that said that she wasn't sure whether or not he should be allowed to be alone with children of any age. He liked that glance. Because he agreed with it. Maybe she'd take the baby home.

Alice. He had to start thinking of her in terms of her name. Alice.

"As for that, there's nothing complicated about changing a diaper. You just want to make sure that you get the diaper area wiped clean, including in all the wrinkles, and there's lots of wrinkles in the baby, without irritating her skin. Some babies have sensitive skin."

"I sure hope Alice doesn't. She needs to take it easy on me."

"We'll find out soon enough. I didn't get any kind of diaper rash ointment or anything like that. But if you need it, I can."

"I feel like you've done more than enough."

"I just want you to know this is counting on my time that I owe you," she said, and there was humor in her voice. Neither one of them were going to actually make her serve that time. She would spend the time with him whether she was forced to or not. Still, it was fun to tease her about it.

"All right. Got it. You're on the clock."

"Good. I hoped I was getting credit for this."

She went on to show him how to change the diaper. It was obvious she was an old hand at it, since she didn't stumble and fumble around the way he was sure he would.

"All right. This outfit seems like it's clean, so I'm putting it back on her, but there were several changes of clothes in the bag. I...didn't even think about getting clothes. What kind of girl am I?"

"The kind of girl who likes dogs and cows and has a lot of compassion in her heart for her friend when he's in a bind."

"All right. I can go with that."

"Good. Because it is true."

Alice had woken up, but she lay with her eyes blinking, looking around.

"I always heard that some babies are more attached to their mothers than others. I would say that if she's fed, with a clean diaper, and you've burped her, and she's still crying, then maybe there's nothing more you can do other than to hold her, although if her crying gets irritating, you can just set her down. It's not going to hurt anything for her to cry."

She lifted her shoulder. "Ashley used to say that to me. When the baby was crying, she would usually hold them, but every once in a while, she would set them down in their crib and walk away from them. She said that she'd done everything she could and maybe he was just overstimulated and needed a little bit of breathing room. Almost every single time, he'd be asleep within ten minutes."

"That's good to know."

"Yeah. There's a lot of baby things that you can get—a swing, bouncer seat, they even have a vibrating bouncer seat now I saw at the store when I was grabbing the formula. But lots of people have raised babies without any of those things."

"I don't know if I'm going to be one of them. It feels like maybe I'm going to need every gadget known to man."

"That's one way to do it." She smiled and then held Alice out, careful to balance her head on her hand while supporting her bottom with the other. "Here you go, Dad," she said softly.

"Wow. I don't think I'm quite adjusted to that."

"I'm sure it's going to take a bit."

He looked up at her, not wanting to ask, but scared to death, and so the words came out. "Will you stay?"

She nodded immediately. "Of course."

He breathed a sigh of relief. "If you're here, I know I can do it."

"That's so funny. You go clear to the underside of the world and spend five years in Brazil, and yet a night in your own house... If I didn't know better, I would think you were making up an excuse just to continue to see me."

"That's possible," he said, very seriously. But she just laughed.

Alice started to whimper, and he was scared that she was going to start wailing again, so he didn't say anything more to Ellen but just tried to bounce the baby gently the way Ellen had been doing.

"I'll make a bottle. Did you use hot water out of the tap?"

He nodded, not taking his eyes off Alice. "That's right."

She made a bottle, and Alice took it, but she didn't go back to sleep.

He and Ellen ended up staying up until five o'clock in the morning, walking the floor with Alice who wouldn't stop crying. He felt terrible, because she was probably missing her mom. And at some point, he figured he would probably just lay her down in her crib and let her sleep, but he didn't want to do that this first night in a strange house with a strange person and none of the things that she was familiar with.

Ellen completely supported him and took turns with him walking the floor with her.

It didn't seem nearly as hard with Ellen beside him. Funny how a good friend could make a hard job easier. He felt bad though, because she got no sleep before she had to leave to teach her aquatics class.

After everything she'd done for him, he knew he owed her big time, but he wasn't sure how he was going to repay her. Especially now that his life had taken such a drastic turn.

Chapter Fourteen

Bernadine used her key to open the aquatic center. She had been coming to water aerobics for over three years. She usually beat the teacher, Ellen O'Riley, and eventually the aquatic center had just given her a key.

That might not be the way normal towns did things, but Sweet Water was a little different. Even though they had an Olympic-caliber training center right in town. Or right outside of town, as the case was.

Regardless, Bernadine ignored the ache in her back and pushed her glasses further up her nose. Her hands were too shaky for her to get her contacts in anymore, and she'd taken to wearing her glasses everywhere. She lost her husband fourteen years before and had celebrated her seventy-fourth birthday just a couple of weeks ago.

She was pretty spry for her age, but she had what the doctors called an essential tremor. They assured her it wasn't Parkinson's, but whatever it was, it made her life a lot more difficult.

She wished she would have appreciated her youth while she had it, because old age stunk. It was hard, and...ever since she'd lost her husband, she wished she had someone to share it with. Surely getting old would be easier if there were two of them to face it together.

But getting married at her age seemed...maybe foolish. It wouldn't be what she wanted, which was a lifetime spent with someone, someone who knew her inside out, could finish her sentences, had seen her at her worst—which would have been childbirth for her or maybe the day her husband had his heart attack. Whichever. Still, someone who had seen her at her worst, knew her foibles and admired her strengths, and covered her weaknesses.

Anyone she met now at her age, they would only have a decade together, or maybe two if they were very blessed. Not long enough at all to know someone the way she'd known her husband.

Still, staying home and crying over spilled milk wasn't going to do her any good either. So, a few years ago, she'd lugged her body off the couch, even though she didn't want to, and had set off to try to find some friends and do something productive with her life.

That's when the aquatic ladies had been born.

She dragged her housemate, rode along with her, and there were a bunch of older and getting older ladies who got their old, creaking bones out of bed before the crack of dawn and came to take a dip in the pool.

Ellen had been faithful in teaching them, and the few times that she had missed, Bernadine had taken over.

Maybe she'd try to start her own aerobics class. She surely ought to be able to do it by now. Being that she was a three-year veteran.

She was in the ladies' locker room starting to change, she had her swimsuit out of her bag, when Ellen walked in, bleary-eyed, looking like she hadn't slept a wink, and making Bernadine think for the first time that maybe the rumors that had been going around about her were true.

"Doesn't look like you slept at all last night," Bernadine said, wondering if she could just come out and ask. She knew older ladies sometimes could get away with things that younger ladies couldn't, but she liked and respected Ellen, and didn't want to spread her secret around town if what she heard last night was actually true.

"Actually, I didn't," Ellen said, looking around the locker room like she'd never seen it before.

"Were you up with the baby?" Bernadine asked, knowing she probably shouldn't have.

Ellen stopped, and the unfocused look in her gaze left immediately and she zeroed in on Bernadine. "How did you know that?" There was wonder in her voice, and total shock.

"That's the rumor that was going around last night. That you'd had a baby, and that you gave it to Travis to raise. That was the reason that he came back from Brazil."

"What about me? Do I get to raise it too?"

"Well, are you?" Bernadine asked, holding her swimsuit in one hand and staring at Ellen. Why in the world would Ellen be asking her?

"I don't know. I... Travis does have a baby, but it's not mine. Not really."

"Well, last time I checked, it took two to create a baby. Of course, with all these newfangled inventions they seem to come out with on a daily basis, maybe there's a way for your phone to pop out a baby that only has a dad and not a mom. Is there?"

Bernadine didn't really think there was, but she never thought that she'd actually be pushing buttons on the screen of a phone and have it do what she told it to do. That was pretty much what her phone did, except when it decided to get cantankerous and not obey her. Or, like her friend said, it was operator error.

Bernadine hated it when it was operator error. After teaching school for forty years, she didn't think she had any operator error left in her, but apparently, she was mistaken.

Ellen shook her head. "No. I did not have a baby." She looked around once more, like she wasn't quite sure where she was again. Which made Bernadine very suspicious. So far, Ellen had been just as good as an adult as she had been in the classroom, but sometimes adults went off the deep end.

"Where's your swimming suit? And your bag?" she asked, narrowing her eyes at Ellen. If there were drugs in her life, Bernadine was going to turn her in. Although, maybe she should have her friends stage an intervention first. Was that what they called it nowadays?

Back in her school days, she'd send the kid to the principal and let him handle it. Not that they ever did, they just sent the kid back to the classroom where they did the exact same thing all over again. Bernadine had finally figured out that if she wanted a problem to be solved, she had to do it herself. A lot of times, the kids who acted up didn't have a good homelife, and she ended up organizing after-school classes for them.

The ones who attended always did better.

But sometimes you just couldn't help people who didn't want to be helped.

"You know what, I totally forgot it!" Ellen said, smacking her forehead and laughing. "I was up all night with the baby."

"The one that's not yours, but Travis's?"

"Yeah. Alice. Her name's Alice, and she is the sweetest little thing."

"Who's the mom?"

"Um. I don't know. I'm not sure he knows her name." Ellen closed her mouth. She looked both ways, maybe to see if any of the other ladies had arrived, and then she lowered her voice to a whisper. "I'm not sure what he's going to say about her. But... Please don't tell anyone. Okay?"

"Tell anyone what? Everybody knows you guys have a baby now."

"That's right. We have a baby."

Ellen gritted her jaw and grimaced, like she hadn't meant to say that, and Bernadine understood, even if she wasn't sure exactly what Ellen was saying, that whatever was going on with the baby wasn't something that they wanted everyone in the town to know.

"Well, you're probably going to need to get it together a little better if you don't want anyone else to be suspicious. I can keep from saying anything, but the ladies who are showing up today have mouths that run like faucets."

"I know." Ellen sighed.

Bernadine felt bad for the girl. She and her husband had never had any children. Maybe that was part of the reason that she felt so alone in her old age. All these choices which seemed like such good choices at the time came back to bite a person as they got older. She had been young and carefree once. She had all of her summers free, and she and her husband had traveled a lot. But now that he was gone, and she was too old to do the things that she used to do, she didn't really have anyone.

So she had to make her own family. It had taken her a while to figure that out though.

Still, Sweet Water was home and felt like family to her, and if Ellen needed her protection, she would give it.

"If you want to go home, I'll teach the class for you today. I can just tell people that you're under the weather, and you can figure out what you want to tell them eventually, but I suggest you not go out and about until you're ready to answer some questions."

"I'm sorry. I really hate to leave you in the lurch, but I can hardly teach without my swimming suit. And..." Ellen looked at her with tired eyes but a grateful smile. "Thanks for the advice. I... I don't want anyone to get hurt."

That seemed like an odd thing to say, but Bernadine nodded, like she understood when she really didn't, and watched as Ellen looked around the locker room again, and then slowly made her way to the door.

"Do you need someone to drive you home?" she asked, usually believing that a person did best if they were made to be responsible, but in this case, Ellen looked so tired Bernadine was actually concerned that she might not make it.

"No. Thank you. I'm fine," Ellen said and walked slowly out the door, greeting Rhoda and Agathe as they walked in, confused when Ellen walked by them, fully dressed, and turned and went toward the outside door.

"She's leaving? Is class cancelled?" Rhoda said as she walked in, her bag slung over her shoulder. Rhoda was younger than many of the other ladies in the group, since she wasn't even to retirement age. She was only sixty years old, but her husband had been some highfalutin surgeon, and after he had died of a heart attack, Rhoda had taken his life insurance and retired comfortably.

She was a sweet lady and one of Bernadine's favorite people. Her two sons were both doctors, and her daughter had become a lawyer. All of them were busy and didn't spend much time with their mother.

Agathe, on the other hand, had moved from France to marry the American with whom she'd fallen in love with on vacation. She had been living in the United States for more than forty years. Her husband had not passed away but was slowly succumbing to Alzheimer's.

"What's going on?" Agathe said in her lilting voice that still held a trace of her French accent.

"Ellen wasn't quite up to snuff, so I'll be teaching the class today,"

Bernadine said, her voice brokering no nonsense. She hadn't learned to control classrooms of thirty thirteen-year-olds by being weak-willed and lily-livered.

"Oh. Well, that's nice," Agathe said, the sadness that never quite left her eyes fading for a bit as they brightened. "I love it when you teach. You do such a good job. Although, I love Ellen as well. Such a sweet girl. About the age I was when I left France." Her voice grew a little wistful.

Bernadine didn't have too much time for dreams and that type of thing, but she knew that Agathe missed her homeland and longed to go back to visit.

She couldn't, however, leave her husband in his condition while she flew all over the globe, not only because it wouldn't look good, but because Agathe was as loyal as a French bulldog and wouldn't dream of leaving the love of her life behind.

It had to be terrible watching him fade away slowly, day by day. It made Bernadine appreciate the fact that her husband had gone quickly. Although it had been a shock and very difficult to get over, she couldn't imagine watching him as he slowly became someone different than the man she fell in love with. When he looked at her and didn't recognize her, when he didn't know the people that they knew, and when carrying on a conversation was impossible. All things that Agathe was almost sure to go through with her husband.

"You know, I heard yesterday that Ellen gave her baby to Travis to raise. I didn't even know she was pregnant," Rhoda said as she struggled into her swimsuit and folded her clothes neatly into a pile.

"Ellen was pregnant?" Agathe said, sounding just as shocked as Bernadine had been.

"You know, with some women, you just can't tell."

"Ladies. We are not going to gossip about Ellen. Ellen has been very good to us, she's never late, she shows up every morning, and she does her very best. Where would we be without her?"

The other two ladies looked at her, thinking about what she said. She knew she was right. Who else wanted to teach a bunch of over-the-hill women water aerobics at five o'clock in the morning?

No one. That's who.

Ellen was one of a kind.

"I think we ought to do something nice for her," Bernadine stated, used to commanding classrooms, except...she had this thought, but she had no idea of what something nice might be.

"What do you suggest?" Rhoda said, willing to go along.

"I don't know. I'm going to need to think about that." She looked at the two of them. "Unless you two have ideas?"

"She loves her dog," Agathe said.

"True that. She also loves her cows. Shaggy, monstrous-looking beasts."

The talk drifted to other things as the other ladies in the class came in, and Bernadine simply announced that she was the teacher that day.

She quashed any hint of anyone trying to mention Ellen and a baby, although it was rather hard. Especially since she didn't know exactly what was going on.

She wished she did, but she wasn't sure who to go to. Regardless, once they got in the water, things eased up and they focused on the various exercises that Ellen always led them through. She did vary them from time to time, and Bernadine simply did a class based on their favorites.

By the time the class was over, she decided that she was going to gather everyone together and discuss it.

At five 'til six, she announced the class was over, but then she said, "If those of you who wouldn't mind listening to an idea I have would stay after class, I'd appreciate it."

"Can we stay in the pool?" Rhoda asked.

"Sure." Bernadine looked around. Typically when they left their class between six fifteen and six thirty, the building was still deserted. Every once in a while, a few athletes who were in training would be showing up about that time, but normally they had things to themselves.

The ladies arranged themselves in a group, some of them moving around in the water and others just swishing their arms back and forth.

There was something very relaxing about water, and she was glad that she had stepped out of her comfort zone and put on a swimming suit for the first time in thirty years; she hadn't regretted it.

Whether or not it made her healthier, as the doctor said it would, she wasn't sure.

"All right, ladies, I've been thinking about something. Periodically in our town, there are people who need help. Now, it's a small town, and everyone's always willing to lend a hand, but the eight of us have been together for years, always coming to class and doing our exercises and leaving. What do you say, instead of just coming to class and doing water aerobics, we could...form a group?"

"What kind of group?" Agathe asked, and if she suspected this had anything to do with Ellen, she didn't say.

Agathe would actually be one of the people that Bernadine thought would need help.

After all, she was going through a hard time, and she shouldn't have to go through it by herself.

"The kind of group who helps people," Bernadine said, and she wanted it to be that simple.

"So we swim, and we...help people?"

"That's exactly right. Now, we need a really cool name." She said "cool," just like the kids did. She figured that probably that word was out of date, like all the other words that had come and gone throughout her lifetime. She was too old to care and definitely didn't need to keep up with them. Back when she was in school, she just had to keep up on the swear words so she could know when a kid needed detention. Beyond that, she couldn't be bothered.

"Does anybody have any ideas?"

"You kind of sprung this on us," Asenath said. "Can't we have a little bit of time to think? Like, until our next class?"

They met three days a week. She supposed she could give them two days to think about a name.

"All right. That is reasonable. We'll take two days to think of a name, and then we'll come back on Wednesday, and we'll decide on a name."

"Who are we going to help? And what are we going to do?"

"Well, I don't know. I just think we should help people. Whether that means giving them things, or staying with them, or—"

"Matching them up with someone. People who are lonely could

find their soulmate in us." Opal looked like she was very proud of herself for coming up with that.

"I don't know if we want to get into that. That's...complicated."

"I think we should vote on it. Isn't that what groups do?" Kitten said slyly.

"All right. We'll vote on it on Wednesday. And we'll vote on a name. Come with your favorite."

She didn't know whether they'd end up helping Ellen or not, but Ellen had given them a reason to band together. And for that, Bernadine was thankful.

Chapter Fifteen

"Are you going to keep her?"

Ford Hansen sat in Travis's living room, staring at the man he'd taken under his wing more than ten years ago. Part of the reason he'd done it was because he wanted to give back to the community, part of it was because of Travis's aptitude, but most of it was because of his wife, Morgan. Actually, almost all the credit should go to Morgan. She had seen something in Ford that no one else had seen, or maybe, she'd just taken the time to draw out the best in him.

He could feel his lips wanting to turn up as he thought about his wife. They'd had more than two decades together and had raised four children. And he loved her more now than he did the day they got married. She was one of those people who did not just put on a show but was truly good from the inside out, truly beautiful in both places.

She'd given up a lucrative career because she hadn't wanted to violate her convictions. He could admire someone like that, and did.

And maybe, that had been God's plan all along, because ultimately, while Morgan was the vehicle that God used, it was God who would reach down for Ford and not allow him to give up on life and become a recluse after his accident.

He resisted the urge to scratch at his eye patch and waited while Travis thought.

"I guess I hadn't really thought I had any other choice," Travis said slowly, as though the idea of not keeping the baby had never dawned on him.

"If that's what you want."

"Maybe that's what I think I need to do," Travis said slowly, as though he were thinking about the words as they were coming out.

"If you think that's what God wants, that's what you need to do." That was always his advice. Sometimes he would tell people to read a certain passage, or passages, in the Bible, particularly if what they thought God wanted them to do violated Scripture. After all, God didn't take the trouble to write the Bible only to tell man to go against it. Therefore, if anyone thought that God was telling them to do something the Bible clearly said not to do, that man was wrong.

But sometimes there were cases where either option would be right from a biblical standpoint. It was at that point in time where a person had to pray, seek the Lord, and then make the choice that they thought God wanted.

"I could report it to authorities, but you know they're going to take the baby from me. And the mom clearly said that she wanted me to raise her."

"You do know people are going to assume that's your baby?"

"I know."

"And I've already heard rumors that they think it's Ellen's baby too. That...could negatively affect her."

"I know. Especially since she's already been here helping me."

Travis had told him that she'd helped him the first long night, and then she stopped in every day afterward. If he had a hard night, she'd watch the baby for a while so he could sleep. Or she'd tidy up his house or watch the baby so he could get some work done. She still had her own work to do, her dogs and her cows and the various things she did around town, but she always made time for Travis.

"I know you want to protect the mom. I know you felt like she was in some kind of danger, but this might be a hard thing for Ellen to shake if people believe she abandoned her own baby."

"I know. I've just not been answering those questions when people ask, because I don't want the fact that there was a baby dropped off here that we don't know who the mom is, that the baby is almost two months old, and have whoever that woman was afraid of tracking the baby down."

"I appreciate you being so protective of her. Someone might want to use the baby for ransom or to hold something over that woman's head. I don't know, but...she could be long gone by now, and Ellen is right here."

"I know. Ellen is...amazing. The best human I know."

"I always thought you...kind of liked her." That was putting things mildly. He always thought Travis had a huge, massive crush on Ellen. In fact, part of the reason Ford had sent him away when he did was because of Ellen's age, because Travis was an adult, and Ellen was only fourteen.

Four years between a couple wasn't much once they became adults, but an eighteen-year-old could not be hanging around a fourteen-year-old with romantic interest.

Travis knew it, but Ford also knew that sometimes teenage boys didn't always act with intelligence. Hormones could be a hard thing to fight.

And Ford didn't want to see Travis end up in prison or branded as a child molester, just because he'd fallen in love with a girl who was too young.

Ford had his suspicions that when Travis fell, it would be forever, and he'd been right about that. Goodness knew that there had never been anyone but Morgan for him. Not since she walked into his house and broke down all his walls, carried away his heart. Of course, with a woman like Morgan, he could trust her with his heart. She'd kept it safe all these years, raised his children, and stood beside him through everything. He would love her until he died.

"I more than kind of like her," Travis finally said, his eyes on the baby who slept cradled in his arms.

"Then it might be a good idea to marry her. She's already spending a lot of time here, helping you with the baby, and if you really don't want to let the baby story get out, that might be the best way to protect Ellen." Normally he wouldn't recommend a marriage happen that quickly, but Travis was as steady as they came. He'd grown as a person, as a businessman. His solid, consistent character had already been in place when he'd been a teenager. And Ellen had a heart of gold. Travis said she was the best human being he knew, and Ford couldn't disagree that she was a wonderful person, who would keep her word if she made vows.

"I didn't want to rush that. I've liked her since before you sent me away." Travis looked up, and for the first time, there was a little humor in his eyes. "Sometimes I wonder if you did that on purpose."

"I guess it's far enough in the past that I can admit that yes, I did."

"Thank you. I probably would have done something I shouldn't have if you hadn't."

"I know." Ford paused. "I don't think less of you. It just wasn't the right time."

"I know. I knew it then. But..." Travis's voice trailed off, and he never finished his thought. Ford could only imagine he was thinking something along the lines of Ellen had been someone he had never been able to resist. That she pulled him like she had a chain wrapped around him and he couldn't get away, could only go closer.

That was how Ford felt about Morgan. He'd like to think that was the way the best marriages were. But everyone had their own love story. It didn't necessarily follow the script. It just needed to be between two people who made vows and meant them. Because, as good as Morgan was, there had been times in their marriage where he hadn't liked her very much. There had probably been more times in their marriage when she hadn't liked him at all. But both of them had stuck with it, and both of them had been determined to see the best in the other.

He thought Travis could have a marriage like that with Ellen, and he had to admire the fact that Travis didn't want to rush it.

"I guess if there's one thing these last few years taught me, it's that... life is short. But at the same time, I've learned patience. Which seems to be a contradiction, but because life is short, you want to savor the things that are really meaningful."

Ford stared at him for a minute, wishing that he had had that kind of maturity at that young of an age. "You know, I think most of the time, people have a tendency to run ahead of God. I think you're on the right track, but I guess I would caution you to make sure that you don't wait too long and miss your opportunity."

To his surprise, Travis's lips pulled back in a slow grin. "That's something else I learned from you. At first, I was too brash, too hotheaded, but as I learned things, I had a tendency to become more deliberate, more thoughtful, slower, and... You know I screwed a few things up because I didn't move quick enough."

"There's a fine line. And maybe staying in touch with the Lord is one of the ways that you're able to walk that line."

"Knowing what God wants, and trying to do it?"

"Yeah. It's not always easy. And..." Ford paused for a second. He knew he was going to say something that maybe wasn't something that every Christian would agree with. But it was something that he felt. "Sometimes I think God just allows us to choose. There is no wrong answer, and He allows us to make the decision. I think maybe sometimes we sweat over decisions that we don't have to. Both are right, so both are good, and either would work."

"I don't know that I've ever thought about it like that before," Travis said.

"Yeah. And like I said, that might not be every decision, and it might not even be true. But whether you keep the baby, whether you give her away. Either one could be a right decision, right?"

"There is no biblical mandate that if somebody drops a baby off, I have to keep it."

"No. And maybe the mandate is to follow the rule of law, and that almost indicates that you should report that to authorities. Except... The mother gave you permission to keep it."

"Right. So either could be right."

"Yeah. I guess I'm just thinking you don't have to feel like you have to keep the baby. And if you think that's what God wants you to do, by all means. Do it. But don't feel guilty if you don't."

"Thank you. I maybe needed that permission. I hadn't even allowed myself to think that I might not keep her. A baby is a big responsibility."

"It is." Ford would know. He'd raised four children of his own with Morgan. He wouldn't go back and change it for the world. His children meant more to him than anything except for his wife and his Jesus. But it wasn't an easy task. Not even for just one child.

"I've been wondering how I can court Ellen the way she deserves, while still taking care of the baby."

Ford nodded, and then he decided to give his opinion on that as well. "Ellen deserves the world. She's a good woman. But... Sometimes the very best women just want you. They don't want all the bells and whistles, they don't want all those special things raining down on them, they just want you. Your time, your attention, you showing them by your words, deeds, actions, whatever it is that speaks to their love language, that she's important to you. And that you love her."

Travis listened. His eyes were narrowed a little, as though he were processing the words as Ford spoke. Travis always listened. That was part of what had made him such a good business protégé. And part of the reason he'd been so successful. He hadn't thought that he knew best, but he'd been willing to be humble and to learn.

He was doing that now, and Ford appreciated it and figured that whatever choice he made, he would be successful in that area of his life as well. After all, a man typically wasn't born a natural romantic.

"I think, I think a lot of times men get things backward. They do all of the pretty shows before the marriage, and then once they're married, they forget to romance their wife. They forget that she chose him, and he chose her, and it takes a certain amount of work to make a marriage relationship work. That after the vows are said is when the real work begins."

"The little bit that I've watched, TV would have us believe the exact opposite."

"Maybe that's why there are so many divorces in the world today." Ford knew that it wasn't that simple. It was mostly because character wasn't valued anymore. Because Christianity was on the decline in America. And what used to be social pressure to stay married had totally disintegrated, and now, anyone who tried to exert any pressure on someone to do right was called judgmental and wrong.

All the stigma of sinning had been removed, and now just like the Bible had predicted, wrong had become right, and right wrong.

Not for the first time, Ford wondered if it had been a smart idea to bring four children into the world, a world that was so twisted and messed up. But until the Lord came back, there was still hope for, if not the entire world, at least individuals. Maybe, maybe because he had brought his children into the world, there would be people who escape the fires of hell and find Jesus, and end up in heaven because of his children. He could only hope so.

That was the point of having children. There might be someone who was saved from the fires of hell because of his child. He was at the point where it could be his grandchildren who pointed someone to Jesus. There was no higher calling.

"Well, she's sleeping, and Ellen will be here soon, so I'm going to head out." They'd already talked about what he'd come to discuss, the investment of the Sweet View Ranch and Travis's exodus from his companies.

Travis had always said that he wanted to move back to Sweet Water and buy property. And he'd worked hard to make that happen. With their joint investment in the Sweet View Ranch, and with the way the Clyborne family was working on it, Travis should be set for life.

"It's always good to see you," Travis said, standing carefully, holding the baby gently so he didn't jerk her as he moved to his feet.

Ford bit back a smile and resisted the urge to scratch his eye patch again. "It's always good to see you too. You might not be working for me anymore, but I'd like to keep in touch, son."

Anytime he'd called Travis son, it had made the younger man beam. This was no exception.

"I can't thank you enough. I really can't."

"Thank Jesus. I am nothing without him."

"Same," Travis said.

Ford held out his hand, and by now, Travis was well used to the fact that he only had three digits on it and gripped it without a second look.

Ford took another peek at the baby and took his leave.

He had a feeling that everything was going to work out for Travis. But from experience, he was pretty sure it wasn't going to be easy.

Chapter Sixteen

Ellen pushed the door open quietly and stepped into Travis's house.

It was quiet, but that didn't necessarily mean it had been a good night. For the last two nights, Alice had been up all night long crying. When Ellen had gotten there in the morning after teaching her aquatics class, Travis had looked like he was ready to drop.

She felt terrible for him but didn't know what to do. Other than to keep coming and giving him a little bit of time to rest while she watched the baby, cooked a meal or two, and did a little bit of cleaning.

They barely talked, because Travis had been so tired.

She tiptoed into the living room, which was where Travis usually crashed if the baby had been up.

She wasn't sure whether he did that so she didn't have to go back to any bedrooms, or whether he just felt more comfortable there. Whichever it was, she appreciated it. She heard the rumors around town that said she was the mother and Travis was the father, and had been asked outright, and had avoided the question as much as she could, which protected the mom of the baby, but it made people very curious about her and her relationship with Travis.

As she walked in, she could see him sitting on the couch, slouched down, with the baby on his chest. He had two pillows beside him, keeping his arm propped up so he formed a little cage with his body so the baby couldn't go anywhere.

She took a moment to just look at him and smile. He'd come so far from the gangly teen that she first knew, becoming a man of character and someone she admired greatly.

"I hope that smile means that you made coffee," he murmured, and she realized that his eyes were open.

"I stopped at the bookstore and grabbed some." She held up the cup she had in her hand.

He drank coffee, while she didn't care for it. But she enjoyed the smell, and she really enjoyed the way it made him smile.

"My favorite."

She nodded. He claimed that he'd been all over the world, but that the coffee in the bookstore at Sweet Water was the best anywhere.

She didn't know if he was just saying that because he loved Sweet Water, or if it was because it was true.

"Hard night?" she asked, although she didn't figure she needed to.

He nodded, shifting up carefully without waking Alice. "She just fell asleep about an hour ago. From experience, I think we can pretty much drop a bomb in the next room and she wouldn't wake up now."

"I'm sorry. I don't think you've had a night of good sleep since she came."

"No. It...makes me understand a little more when people say how parenting is so hard. Is such a sacrifice. I don't think she's going to be appreciating this anytime soon."

"Probably in another thirty or forty years," Ellen said with a small laugh. She didn't really remember her own mom, but she must have stayed up overnight with her. Must have fed her when she was hungry, changed her, and put cute little dresses or outfits on her.

"What's that look for? I feel like I lost you."

He always noticed. Even when she didn't want him to. Not really. Although, she did want to share those memories or thoughts of her mom.

"I guess I was just thinking about my mom. I don't really remember her at all, but she must have stayed up with me. I suppose at this point in time, I'm ready to thank her for it, but... I don't even remember."

"That's sad. You had a mom who cared, whom you can't remember, and I had a mom who didn't care, and I remember her all too well."

That made her heart clench, and she wanted to go over and sit down beside him. Take his hand in hers, and somehow cover the ache that must be in his chest over the fact that his mom never really seemed like she liked him very much.

"Although, she did kind of give me a gift with that."

"She did?" Ellen asked, walking over and handing him his coffee instead.

"Yeah. You don't know how many times in the last couple weeks since Alice came that I thought to myself, if somehow I managed to survive the neglectful care that I know my mother gave me, surely I can't really do anything that's going to hurt Alice."

"I guess that's one way of putting a positive spin on it." Leave it to Travis to find the good in it.

He nodded.

"Here. Let me take her, and you can have a little bit of peace and quiet time."

That was usually the extent of their conversations, because by the time he would get up, she would be ready to leave.

But he shook his head this morning while slowly straightening. Moving the baby down so she was cradled in his arms, he stood with his coffee in one hand and the baby in the other. She almost made a joking comment about how he'd gotten really good.

She didn't, because she was too busy wondering. Maybe he heard the rumors and was going to tell her to go home. That he could handle it by himself from now on.

He had the pack and play still set up in the living room, although she had gone to the store the second day he had Alice and bought the crib. That was set up in the spare bedroom. The one that used to be the boys' room.

He set the coffee on the end table and put Alice down in the pack and play gently, tucked her blanket around her, and straightened.

"I've been so tired, it's been so...hard. With the baby, coming in and trying to get settled, and rearranging all the plans I had for when I hit the ground here in Sweet Water. I haven't had a chance to thank you."

"You don't need to thank me." Was that all he wanted? She didn't need a big production. She was here because...he was a friend and she... loved him.

"Maybe I just wanted to."

"Okay. You're welcome." She shrugged her shoulders, thinking it wasn't that big of a deal.

He took a look at Alice, as though to make sure she'd not woken up after being set down, then he closed the distance between them.

"No. You deserve more than that. You deserve...everything." His words were slow, as though he were struggling to find them, but her tongue was stuck to the roof of her mouth and she couldn't have helped him if she wanted to as he stepped closer, putting a hand on her shoulder.

She forgot to breathe.

She couldn't swallow. Her throat was too dry. She waited.

A soft feeling. Light touch. Dark look, hooded but sincere. She couldn't tear her eyes away. Had trouble remembering her name, and without realizing it, her hand came up and touched his waist.

"Ellen," he murmured.

Because she touched him? Because he wanted to talk to her? She wasn't sure. Just knew that the way he said her name made her feel like he cherished her, which was crazy. It was just a name. A sound in the air. He hadn't done anything.

Their breath mingled, the only sound in the room, as they stood like that, his hand on her shoulder, hers at his waist, and stared into one another's eyes.

"Do you remember that night?" he finally murmured.

She tried to swallow so she could talk, but her throat wouldn't work. She nodded her head. She knew exactly what he was talking about. The night he left.

"I wanted to kiss you so bad. Wanted to stay." His hand came up and touched her cheek, running the backs of his fingers softly down her skin, his breath shallow and ragged. "I never wanted anything so much in my life before."

She, as young as she was, had wanted it too.

"The best thing for you was for me to leave. I know, I know I could have gotten in trouble. That really wasn't the heaviest thing on my mind. It was you. You needed more years."

It was true. She had been too young. He had made the right decision by walking away, but that had been ten years ago. Why had he stayed away? That was what she didn't understand. That was what made her feel like he'd changed his mind.

There were a thousand, a million ways he could have let her know he wanted her. But he didn't and he hadn't, and she set her heart on being friends. The best friend she could be.

"I don't think I've ever done anything harder than walking away from you that night."

"I didn't want you to."

"That was part of what made it so hard. I knew that."

Maybe she should be embarrassed of that. She hadn't realized her feelings were so transparent.

"It doesn't feel like the right time to tell you this now. It wasn't the right time then, then there was more for me to learn, then Ford wanted me to go to Brazil. There just never seemed to be the perfect time for me to tell you how I feel." His eyes dropped to her lips, and his finger traced across the skin just beneath them, and she resisted the urge to pull them in and bite them.

"So I decided I was going to make the time." A small smile lifted his lips but didn't show his teeth. "Last night, Alice was crying, screaming, and I was thinking about my mother. How much I would have loved to have had a tender word from her, a soft touch, some kind of sign that I was more to her than just a strange kid who happened to hang out at her house a lot."

"That hurts my heart to hear that."

"This is not about that." He shook his head, like he wanted to get past that, didn't want her dwelling on that. "But I thought about how short life is. How many opportunities she had, but maybe it didn't feel like the right time to her. Maybe she really wasn't thinking of me, or maybe... I don't know. But I didn't want to let another day go by without me telling you how much you mean to me. I didn't want...

things happen. You could be gone tomorrow. I could be gone tomorrow—"

"Don't say that!"

"It's true. One day we're here, the next day we're not. Our life is a vapor. And I didn't want to live my life or to have you live yours, to lose you without ever telling you that I love you. I've loved you since you were a skinny teen, hauling your cow around everywhere, with your dog as your best friend."

"I was fat."

"No, you weren't." His brows drew down, like somehow he'd never noticed?

"Chubby. I was chubby."

"I don't care. I never paid attention to that."

"It didn't feel like it. It felt like...like there were cheerleaders who caught your eye."

"And you waited for me to get some sense. I wasn't perfect."

"I didn't expect you to be."

"I didn't see you like that for a while. You were a lot younger. But... you were faithful. Faithful in a way that no one else in my life has ever been. Maybe that's what drew my attention to you to begin with, but I fell in love with you at some point, and I've never fallen back out. Ever." He pressed his lips together and blew the breath out of his nose as he lifted his eyes and looked over her shoulder as though deciding whether or not to say more. "I've been faithful to you since that day in the barn. The day that I wanted to kiss you, but didn't and walked away instead."

She blinked. Trying to process what he was saying. She... She wondered over the years. Maybe he'd left because he had girlfriends. Maybe he hadn't stayed because he changed his mind. Maybe she was just friendship material while there were other girls that were...more.

He didn't need to say this now. Didn't need to tell her everything, didn't need to discuss the time that elapsed between them. If he wanted to, he could just pick up from today.

But he wanted her to know that he'd been faithful. To her.

"I wondered what you've been doing. All the times you were away. But we didn't talk about it for a long time. You never mentioned anyone, but that didn't mean there weren't people, women."

"No. Occasionally I had to take a date to a business party or lunch or something, and Ford usually found someone for me. I think he tried to find people who would never be interested in a skinny kid, since my dates always seemed to be older women who were interested in someone else."

"I'll have to thank him," Ellen murmured. Not sure what direction Travis was going with this conversation, but the fact that he was touching her, telling her he was faithful to her, talking about the time he almost kissed her, and didn't. He'd said he loved her, but maybe he was talking about as a friend.

"Yeah. I have a lot of things to thank Ford for." He bent down, kissed her forehead, just a gentle touch of his lips on her skin, and she closed her eyes as he stayed there, like he just wanted to be close enough to touch her, to catch her scent, to feel her heat.

She remembered the little boy he'd been and how he longed for his mother's touch, and maybe he just needed that closeness. Or maybe it was something more.

"It was a lonely ten years, and I never asked you to wait for me. I didn't want you to not be with someone, just because you promised. It took a lot of faith, but I wanted you to want me enough to wait. Without me asking. I thought to myself that if that happened, then when I got home... Maybe it meant you felt for me exactly what I felt for you."

"You know I've been faithful. If I hadn't been, everyone in town would be talking about it." He snorted a little at her words. "And the fact that a baby shows up, and everyone assumes that if it was yours, it was mine."

"I guess that was all I needed to know."

"But I hate those assumptions. After the struggle to do right, to be what the Lord wanted, that everyone would just assume that we hadn't, it's frustrating."

"It's good for the baby. And it was good for my heart. I shouldn't admit that, and I know that it shouldn't feel as good as what it did, but the last ten days as I listened to the rumors, every time I hear that people think it's yours, and they think I'm the father, it just makes me smile.

There's never been another name associated with you, and...that just really makes me feel good."

"It wasn't on purpose. It was just, there just wasn't anyone else who compared. Ever. For anything."

"That's hard for me to believe. I'm not that great of a person."

"You are to me. You've grown into a better one since the boy I knew walked away."

There was silence for a bit, and she thought maybe he was just enjoying the closeness. She brought her other hand up and slid her hands around his back. He let out a groan but didn't move. Almost like he was afraid to.

"Do you think you could love the man I've become?" There was a bit of anguish in his voice that broke her heart.

"I do! I love the boy you were, and I love even more the man you are now." How could she tell him how her heart turned over when she saw him holding Alice? She lifted her head, and he pulled back a bit to give her room. She took one finger and traced the bruise that was fading from his eye, the scab that had healed up on the edge of his jaw, where the edges were red and painful looking.

"You didn't have to come back and have a fistfight for me. I would have gone willingly."

He grinned a little, and maybe she shouldn't have tried to lighten the air at all, but she didn't like the anguish she'd heard, like telling her what he felt was painful.

But she also understood that he hadn't had a whole lot of love in his life. That having feelings for someone almost always involved pain for him and weren't usually returned.

That loving her was a risk for him. No matter how rich or successful he had become, a person's childhood never really faded completely away, and the idea that she might reject him probably loomed large in his head.

She couldn't fix any of that stuff. She couldn't take his childhood away and give him a happy one instead. She couldn't make anything in the past better.

She realized now that she had probably done the best thing that could possibly have been done for him when she'd been faithful, even though he hadn't asked. Even though he hadn't been around, even though he hadn't kissed her before he left and declared his feelings.

If that didn't convince him that she loved him, she figured there probably wasn't a whole lot that would.

"You know I'd do that again, as bad as it hurt."

"Of course. Because that's the kind of man you are. I know you didn't want to."

His smile said that he appreciated the fact that she acknowledged that. That he wasn't bloodthirsty and didn't have an ax to grind or any kind of male posturing to prove. That the fight had been for her.

"I love you," he said, still smiling.

"I love you too," she said simply.

"It's hard for me to believe."

She lifted her brows.

"But I do. Mostly because you waited. You were faithful. You didn't give up on me, find someone else, and walk away."

"No. I've got a feeling that in this lifetime, you're the only man for me. So take care of yourself."

"Maybe I'll just let you do that."

"Well, I have a tendency to be clumsy. And I come with some cows."

"Don't forget about Chewy."

The dog whined at their feet, and they both looked down and smiled.

"I don't want to think about it, but Chewy is getting older, and she's not going to be with me forever, but...you are."

"Yeah." His eyes rested on her arms, still dark, still swirling with the motion. "So about that night when I walked away?"

"Yeah?"

"I don't think there's a day that's gone by that I didn't pray that I'd get a second chance."

"A second chance?"

"To kiss you."

"Oh." Her fingertips started to tingle.

"How about now?"

"Now? I don't think so."

He lifted his chin, his lips pressed together, his eyes showing disappointment, and a little confusion, and maybe pain at what he perceived as her rejection.

"You waited too long. It's my turn. I'm kissing you."

He let out a breath, laughing a bit, and then he stood still. "All right. That's fair. I can give you that."

"Good. Because I was going to take it even if you didn't give it."

"Really?"

"Because you said you loved me. I feel like kissing is part of that."

"I feel like you might be right."

But maybe that wasn't the way to go about it. "I think I'm wrong."

"What do you mean?"

"Maybe, maybe it should be both of us. Not just you. Not just me. Both of us."

"Yeah. You're right. I have a feeling something like kissing is better done together."

They were both smiling as his head lowered, and she closed her eyes, feeling like an eternity slipped by between each second as his arms tightened around her and she waited for his lips to touch hers.

Her fingers fisted at the back of his neck as their lips met, and the boy of her dreams became the man in front of her, kissing her, holding her, loving her.

Chapter Seventeen

"Thanks so much for coming. See you guys on Friday," Ellen said as she used a towel to dry her arms and looked at the ladies who were still in the pool.

Agathe knew she needed to get out. Her husband, Jim, would be waiting at home. Whether he was waiting for her or for someone that he knew only in his mind, she wasn't sure. In other words, she didn't know whether he would be having a good day, and remember her, or a bad day, and have no idea who she was, getting upset when she went in the kitchen and started to make him breakfast.

So far, he hadn't gotten violent with her, but a couple of times, he scared her.

His decline had been slow and heartbreaking.

"All right, ladies. I've given you more time than I originally expected and I warned you a couple weeks ago that we were going to take a vote. Today is the day. Are you going to be in the group?" Bernadine spoke with authority from the corner of the pool where she treaded water.

Agathe moved over to the ladder, one hand on it, her feet firmly on the floor. The last thing she needed was to have some kind of accident. Who would take care of her husband if she was laid up? Who would take care of her?

"I wish I could," she said, making her voice sound as American as possible. The French from her childhood was always on the tip of her tongue, although it had been many years since she had stopped dreaming in French and English had become the language of her thoughts and dreams. Rightfully so, since America was her adopted country, although sometimes she longed for her homeland with an ache she couldn't describe. An ache Jim wouldn't understand, as patriotic as he felt about America.

"But I just can't. My husband needs me right now."

She pressed her lips together, while Bernadine looked at her.

"You are a special exception. I understand, your husband comes first. There will always be a spot on our team for you."

Bernadine sometimes forgot that she wasn't speaking to a classroom full of thirteen-year-olds anymore. She'd done it for so long that she had a tendency to treat everyone the way she would a junior-high child.

Agathe just nodded. "Thanks. I really would love to have the time to reach out more and do more for other people." It wasn't that she lived a life only for herself, but just getting out of the house right now felt like a major victory. She could only come early in the morning, since she couldn't chance leaving later and having Jim wander off.

Soon, she figured sooner than she wished, she would no longer be able to skip out of the house at all.

"Agathe?" Bernadine said in her no-nonsense voice.

"Yes?" she asked as she put one foot on the ladder and began to climb out of the pool.

"You'll let us know if you need help, okay?"

"Of course," she said, but she wouldn't. How could she ask her friends to come and see the decline of her husband? He wouldn't want them to, and she... As much as she would love to have help, she felt like it was her responsibility to take care of him. She'd pledged her life to him, left her country for him, bore his children, and helped him bury his parents and two siblings. She couldn't desert him now. It was her job to take care of him.

She held off while listening to Bernadine talk to the other ladies and decide on a name for their group.

It was a neat name, and it made Agathe smile. Smile and wish that she were a part of it, but knowing that she just couldn't.

She didn't want to resent Jim. He'd been good to her through the years, although regardless of whether he'd been good or not, her first duty was to her husband. She wasn't confused about that.

Although sometimes, when he didn't even remember who she was, she wondered how much longer she could continue to do this on her own.

Maybe she would have to try to find someone to help, but healthcare was expensive, and she hardly thought that she could afford it.

Changing her clothes, she put her suit in the plastic bag she brought for that purpose and put it in her bag. Hurrying out to her car, grateful that it wasn't the dead of winter, which made getting around so much harder, she drove the short distance to Sweet Water and her home.

At first, she smiled as she saw that Jim was up and out, standing on the porch. Her happiness turned to dismay as she realized that all he was wearing was his underwear.

She supposed she should be happy that he even had that on, since once she caught him in the backyard completely naked, and when she confronted him, he had no idea how he got there and hadn't even realized that he was naked and outside.

That was just what she needed, a neighbor to report them for indecent exposure. She didn't know if she could explain to the authorities that Jim really didn't know what he was doing sometimes.

Maybe it was time to have him committed to a facility that was meant to take care of that type of patient.

She didn't want to do that though.

"Jim. Darling. Aren't you cold?"

"Who are you?" he asked, squinting at her with his brows drawn. He hadn't thought to put on his glasses before he went out. Maybe he'd forgotten he even wore glasses.

Her heart squeezed. He'd been so dashing when she'd fallen in love with him. So confident, an arrogant US airman on vacation in the south of France. How could she not be flattered and excited when his attention had fallen on her, a little country girl from France? An unassuming girl from the country who had no hopes of ever being noticed by a handsome, older man.

Their courtship had been a whirlwind, although the red tape she had to go through to get a visa and immigrate to the United States had not been a whirlwind. It had been a major headache, but Jim had stood by her through everything, loving her and wanting her. No matter how hard their governments made it for them to be together.

"I'm Agathe, your wife."

"I'm not married." Jim looked down at his hand and saw the wedding ring she'd put there four decades ago. "Who put this on my finger?"

"I did. Forty-three years ago."

Jim looked back up at her, his brows drawn down mulishly, but he didn't argue. It was obvious he had no clue.

"I think maybe we better go inside and get some clothes on you."

"No."

It wasn't nearly as cold out as North Dakota would get, but she needed to think of something to say to get him in.

"You don't want me to go in your house by myself, do you?"

She prayed it worked as he continued to stare at her, not moving.

Finally, he looked around and said, "I told my friends I didn't want them to leave me, and they've gone off and left me with you. I don't know where you came from, but you better not have stolen any of my stuff."

"I wouldn't steal any of your things, darling." She tried to keep the sadness out of her voice, and the hurt. She knew he didn't mean it. He didn't know what he was saying. The Jim that she lived with all of these decades loved her, totally adored her, practically worshiped the ground she walked on. He'd always treated her like she had been a precious jewel that he had found in a foreign country. And she had never had any doubt that his love was true.

She supposed that made it easier to take care of him, but it made it harder to hear things like that. Things he never would have said to her if the terrible disease that was marching through his brain wasn't altering his personality.

"I've been lied to before. I'm going to report this to my superiors," he muttered to himself as he turned around and stood at the door, waiting for her to open it for him.

Her Jim, the Jim she'd been married to for forty years, would never have allowed her to open a door in his presence.

He'd babied her, cherished her, loved her, and taken care of her for years. It was the least she could do to do it for him now.

Lord, please give me strength.

Chapter Eighteen

"My goodness, how she's grown," Claudia said as Ellen walked out of the post office in Sweet Water.

"I know. She's getting heavy," Ellen said, putting an arm of support under Alice, where she hung from the carrier attached to the front of Ellen. It had been almost a month that Travis had been taking care of her. And she really had changed in a noticeable way, losing some of her newborn look and looking more like a chubby little baby.

"How are you?" Claudia said, and Ellen realized that they had never gotten together to chat. She had promised that, but there had been so many things happening that she just hadn't made the time.

"I'm doing well. She was up a lot last night, which means that Travis was up with her, and when I come during the day, I often take her with me whenever I have to go somewhere so that he can have some time to rest."

"That's awfully nice of you," Claudia said, and there didn't seem to be any censure or disappointment in her voice. But Ellen felt like she needed to explain anyway.

"I'm sorry that we never made it to get together. I... I've been pretty busy."

"You don't have to explain. You don't owe me anything. Although, if you ever want to talk, I certainly am willing to listen. I'd like to actually."

"I hope someday that the story can be told. I think that there may be some danger for people if it gets out right now."

"I understand," Claudia said, and she didn't seem the slightest bit offended that she couldn't be privy to the information. After all, Ellen knew that Claudia wouldn't say anything if she asked her not to. But if she told one person, then another, then another, then soon the whole town would know, and there wasn't any point in trying to keep it a secret.

Not that she thought that that was necessarily the right thing to do.

She and Travis hadn't had a chance to talk since the morning that he told her that he loved her for the first time.

It hadn't been that long ago, and Ellen still hadn't come down from the glow that those words and that confession had given her.

And that kiss.

Definitely the glow was most likely from the kiss.

She smiled.

"Well. That's a...very nice smile," Claudia said with a wink.

"Hey, polecat. How are things going out there on Polecat Lane?" Jesper Hansen stepped out of the post office, and Ellen turned to greet him, but his eyes were only for Claudia.

It was no secret in town that Claudia and Jesper never got along. Which was a little bit odd, considering that the Hansen family was well-beloved in town, and Claudia's family, the Clybornes, got along with everyone.

But she supposed that sometimes there were just people who rubbed each other the wrong way.

"Look who got out of the pigsty long enough to go to the post office. I sure hope you took your monthly shower before you did so. Oh, I guess not," Claudia said, her words sweet but her eyes throwing daggers at Jesper as she waved her hand below her nose like there was a stench in the air.

"Sorry, polecat. That smell is from you."

"If that's what you want to think, go ahead. That doesn't make it true," Claudia called to his retreating back.

"Ugh! That man makes me so angry," Claudia whispered to Ellen as she stomped her foot on the sidewalk and crossed her arms over her chest.

Ellen opened her mouth to ask what had happened all of those years ago that had caused such a problem between them. She'd tried to ask before and just had never been able to get the words out. They didn't come any easier this time either, and before she could say anything, a furry head stuck itself between Ellen and Claudia.

"Billy," Ellen said as she put a protective hand around the sleeping Alice, just so Billy's horns didn't accidentally bump her, and petted Billy with her other hand, scratching him on the forehead and down around his cheek to where he loved it under his chin.

"Oh my goodness. Sweet Water is so unique," Claudia said, one hand on Billy and the other scratching Munchy who had come up beside her.

Billy had been chasing Munchy for years, and finally she seemed to have given up, or maybe Billy finally won her over, but for the last few years, they'd been together.

"I know Lark keeps trying to keep these two on her farm, and of course Jeb indulges her, because Jeb indulges Lark with whatever she wants, but he can't seem to stay away from town."

"As I understand it, they'd been fed in town for years. If it were me, I wouldn't want to give that up either."

"I guess that's a good point. And you're right. For a long time, the town took care of them. Billy was known as a matchmaking steer, and Munchy seemed to be his accomplice, although I think the love affair was really between those two."

"I think they're just good friends. They're not romantic partners or anything, they just...love each other."

"Yeah. Like friends do." Although, her friendship blossomed into more. And she couldn't say that she was upset about that. It actually made her smile every time she thought about it. Although, Munchy and Billy would never be anything but friends. Still, a good friendship was a great way to start a relationship of more.

Of course—she eyed Claudia—sometimes enemies could turn into lovers as well.

"I better get back. I parked my car around back, and I left Travis sleeping. He's not going to know where we went, because I forgot to write a note. You know how hard it is to juggle the baby and a baby bag and all of the paraphernalia that you have to take whenever you go out somewhere? Even some place as simple as the post office."

"I have to take your word on that, I have eleven siblings, but I'm one of the younger ones, so I don't have the war stories that the older kids have of taking care of us younger ones."

"You have nieces and nephews, though."

"A couple," Claudia said, and she didn't say anything more.

With losing their parents, and then selling the family farm, and moving to Sweet Water, and trying to get the ranch up and running and making enough money to support all twelve of them, no one in the family had had much time to get married.

Not because folks in Sweet Water hadn't been trying to marry them off. For years, the Peacemakers had been a matchmaking group in Sweet Water, but most of the ladies had finally hung up their hats, or crafting supplies as the case was.

One, June, had moved away.

They waved goodbye to each other, and Ellen walked around the post office, humming softly to herself.

It was true, having a baby was a lot more work than what she had ever figured. But every day, she fell in love with Alice just a little bit more. As far as she knew, Travis hadn't decided for sure what he was going to do about her. The main thing had been to get her settled in and make sure that she was being properly taken care of.

He might have mentioned in passing that he thought that maybe her mother would come back around, but she never had. At least so far.

He could hardly adopt her without her mother's permission. And he couldn't really do much of anything without her giving him at least guardianship rights.

More than that though, Ellen wasn't sure where she and Travis were headed together. Not that it mattered, she'd go wherever he wanted, just...she wanted to talk about it and get things straightened away or at least planned out.

Calling Chewy, who jumped up from where she lay in the shade of the post office, falling into step beside her, she walked around the building and toward her car.

Chewy jumped in and lay down in the back seat while Ellen struggled to figure out the front carrier. Taking Alice out and getting her in her car seat without waking her up was quite an accomplishment and took a little bit of finagling.

As Ellen latched the final buckle of the car seat and straightened, reaching to close the car door, a woman she didn't know jumped in the driver's door.

"Hey! What are you doing?" She was too shocked to move for a moment before she realized that the lady was starting her car.

The tattoos on her neck looked familiar, as well as the dark hair, and the tattoo sleeves on both arms.

"Hey! I know you!"

The lady had the car started and looked back over her shoulder as she yanked it into drive. "Get out my way!"

Maybe it was Ellen's imagination, but the lady paused for just a moment, as she seemed to recognize Ellen, before she slammed her foot down on the gas.

Ellen didn't have time to run around the car. The car started moving, and Ellen did the only thing she could think of. She threw herself in the passenger window which was thankfully down. Her air conditioning didn't work, and her car was such an old clunker that she never thought that anyone would even think about stealing it. Of course, it was Sweet Water, and everyone left their keys in the ignition, especially if they were just going to the post office.

Ellen had never thought anyone in their right mind would try to steal it.

Ellen struggled to get the lower half of her body in the car as the woman shouted at her, "Get out! Get out!"

"Stop," Ellen said, trying to dodge the woman's hand as she stiff-armed Ellen, trying to push her back out the window.

"You're the mother of this baby!" Ellen said, wanting the woman to know she recognized her. Did she steal the car on purpose? Had she been following Ellen around, waiting for the opportunity to take her baby back?

"I didn't mean to take your car!" the woman said, and then she started to sob as she careened around the hardware store, shot out the alley, and bounced into the street, swerving around Billy who stood looking at her, placidly chewing his cud like a carjacking was something that happened every day, and nothing could faze him.

"Pull over. You don't need to take my car. If you need something, I'll help you," Ellen said, feeling like it was obvious, but some people just defied logic. After all, if the woman could take her baby to Travis, and Travis took care of it without saying anything, surely she could ask him for help if she needed a car.

Ellen finally managed to get her feet in the window, although she had to hold on tight as the woman jerked the wheel, taking them down the lane past the diner, then jerking it again to go around the block, coming back out on the main street, and flipping in the opposite direction, screeching the tires as she yanked the wheel, dodging the newly planted trees along the sidewalk and a recycling bin.

Ellen sat up in time to see Billy calmly watching them leave.

The steer hadn't moved a muscle, other than his mouth as he chewed his cud.

He looked just as content as always, and Ellen figured maybe that was what happened with old age. A person got more content to watch and didn't feel the need to get excited about things.

As it was, she was plenty excited.

"Would you please stop?" she said.

"I'll stop if you promise that you get out and I'll never see you again," the woman said.

"You need help. How could I not help you?"

"Because no one helps me." There was bitterness all through her voice.

It made Ellen stop and think. She'd been blessed. She had...not parents, but her uncle had stepped up to be a dad, and the woman he married had treated her like a daughter. She had a family who loved her. And she'd never doubted it. She thought of Travis, who had never felt like he had a family who loved him. Maybe this woman felt the same. She just hadn't had someone like Ford come into her life and help her out.

Or maybe, maybe she just made bad choices. Sometimes a person could only trace their misery back to themselves.

They passed the sale barn at the edge of Sweet Water, and Ellen glanced over at the speedometer. She was going more than eighty miles an hour. Ellen was kind of impressed since she hadn't realized her car could go that fast.

"Would you please be careful? Alice is in the back seat."

"I know. This is just my luck. I have to be the stupidest person in the world. I finally found someone who could take care of my child, do a good job at it, and I have to go and pick the one car that my kid is in. Man, can anyone possibly be stupider than I am?"

"Well, I could maybe give you some stories about some things that I've done that have been pretty dumb, but I don't think I could top this." Ellen didn't figure that there was any point arguing with her. After all, if you're trying to give your kid up, then you hijack a car with your kid in it, yeah. That...pretty much took the cake for shooting yourself in the foot.

"Thank you. You would make a great counselor," the woman said, sarcasm heavy in her voice.

"Thanks. I'm Ellen by the way." She held her hand over, noticing that the woman had slowed down to seventy-five. Or maybe her car was just getting tired.

Ellen prayed a little that she wouldn't take her hand off the wheel to shake, but manners were ingrained, and she couldn't not offer her hand.

"I'm Alaska," the woman said, offering her hand but only taking her eyes off the road for a second. "I'm pretty sure that typical carjacking etiquette does not require me to introduce myself to the car owner and shake her hand. I'll have to check the manual."

Ellen stared at her for a moment. Then she laughed. "You just made a joke."

"Yeah. My sense of humor shows up at the oddest times." The woman rolled her eyes. And that's when Ellen knew that this could be the start of a beautiful friendship.

Chapter Nineteen

"Did you not realize that it was your daughter that I was putting in the back seat?" Ellen had that question on the tip of her tongue for a while as they had been careening down the road. She didn't know how else to ask it other than just letting it come out. Alaska seemed to be a nice person. Funny that she'd be in Sweet Water, stealing a car. It made more sense to Ellen that she would be in Sweet Water to get a glimpse of her baby.

Her question made Alaska sigh and some of the starch that had been in her back seemed to drain out as she slumped a bit.

"No. I didn't."

"Wasn't she the reason you were in Sweet Water?" Ellen asked, and she tried to make her words sound gentle. She wasn't trying to accuse Alaska of anything. While she had never gone down some of the roads Alaska obviously had, she knew it was only because God had blessed her with her uncle Tadgh. After all, she had lost her mother at an early age. She could easily have gone off the rails, being shuffled from relative to relative, or even have ended up in some kind of foster care situation, whatever Ireland had to take care of children who lost their parents and didn't have family who would take them in, since that was where she was at the time.

"A little," Alaska said evasively.

"You don't have to tell me if you don't want to," Ellen said, hoping Alaska would decide she would trust her, but knowing she couldn't make her.

They drove a bit in silence, with Alaska slowing the car down to five miles an hour under the posted speed limit. Something Ellen noted with gratitude. So far, Alice had been quiet in the back, but...her safety was the most important thing.

"I knew I was less likely to get caught in Sweet Water. That's part of the reason I dropped Alice off there. I knew it was a good town. And I knew Travis is a good man."

"How do you know him?" Ellen asked immediately, trying not to be jealous. Travis had been faithful. He said so. And she trusted him. But, he definitely knew people she didn't, including this woman, apparently.

"I knew his mom. I saw him sometimes in the bar begging her to go home. Trying to get her to step up to her responsibilities. At the time, I thought it was cute, but stupid."

She sighed, tapping the steering wheel with one black-painted fingernail. "Still, that's not the type of thing a person forgets, and when I found myself in a situation where I needed someone I could depend on to take care of my daughter, Travis was the person I thought of first."

"So that's why you said his brother was the father?"

She snorted. "It wasn't hard to figure out that he wasn't anywhere around to deny my claim. And that's the best kind of person to blame fatherhood on. Someone who's not there to defend himself." She laughed without humor.

Ellen could see the logic there.

"The only problem is, modern-day communication is much better than you think it would be. The brothers were talking. I kind of hoped that either they wouldn't be able to get in touch, or they wouldn't be talking to each other, or that Travis would be so upset at his brother he wouldn't have allowed him to give his side of the story."

A miscalculation on that last thought especially. She'd underestimated Travis, and his desire to keep his family together.

Ellen smiled. Just the thought of Travis being... Travis. Upright, conscientious, and determined to do right, made her feel good inside.

He loved her. For herself. And not only did that make her feel good, but the memory of his kiss, the way he held her, and how safe and cherished she felt, was enough to make her forget that she was riding in the car with a woman she'd never met before, and needed to keep her wits about her if only to get Alice out of the backseat somewhere safe.

"I know your problems aren't simple," she began slowly.

That elicited another, rather loud, snort from Alaska.

"But, I know that you'd have a safe place to stay if you wanted to turn the car around and go to Travis's house."

"That's a problem with all of you goody-goody's. You think life is so easy." There was obvious bitterness in Alaska's tone.

"No. I... I don't know what you need my car for, but at the very least, I know you love your child, since you went through so much trouble to find a good home for her."

"I do." Alaska didn't say anything more, but her words were soft, full of longing.

That made Ellen think that maybe she really did want a better life, and maybe she really didn't know how to go about getting it. Of course, Ellen had no idea of the problems she was facing, and maybe she really couldn't help, but she couldn't not offer.

"At the very least, you can turn this around and let me get Alice out of the car." She took a breath, and then plunged ahead. "I don't know where you're taking us, but surely you prefer for Alice to be with Travis."

"So you'd be okay if I dropped Alice off, and you'd stay in the car with me?" She seemed to be saying that as a challenge.

"I prefer to get out with Alice, but if you wanted me to stay, I would do it, as long as you allow Alice to go."

"I think you would have made a good mother for her. If I'd known you before I knew Travis, I might have dropped her off with you."

"If things go the way I hope they do, I might end up being her mother."

"You love Alice that much?" Alaska almost seemed to forget to look at the road, and her eyes ran over Ellen's face as though trying to figure out whether her words were sincere or not.

"I do love Alice, and so does Travis. But... Travis has been my best friend for a really long time, and I think we might be more." She could feel her cheeks heating a little. The way he kissed her certainly seemed to indicate more than friends. The things they talked about did so as well.

"Well. Of all the ironic things that could happen, I end up kidnapping Travis's girlfriend."

"And your own daughter," Ellen said, figuring that was the most ironic thing of all.

"Yeah." Her word was soft, like she was thinking of all the things she regretted, and wishing she could do things over again.

"You know, maybe that's not just the universe playing tricks on you." Ellen started out slowly knowing that what she had to say might not be welcomed by Alaska.

"Really? Is there any other explanation?"

"God wants you. That's my explanation."

A derisive snort was her only answer as her knuckles whitened on the steering wheel.

"You can laugh. But, you have to admit that the odds of this happening are astronomically low. So low that I would almost say that they were impossible. Except, with God anything is possible. And maybe, maybe you ended up with your baby, and me, because God's trying to get your attention."

"Yeah. I don't want Him to want me and what for, anyway?"

She didn't say anything more, just kept driving.

Ellen sat for just a moment. She wasn't any good at this. She never had the words to say, and they sounded trite and insincere almost when they came out of her mouth. But, it really did seem like God might be chasing after Alaska, and He was prompting her to do something about it. For some reason, although God was quite capable of doing anything He wanted to, He used man to accomplish his will.

"Maybe he's trying to get your attention, maybe he wants you, because he loves you."

"That's rich. I don't know why He would."

"Because he created you." Ellen didn't allow her to say anything, but plunged ahead. "The same way you love Alice. After all, Alice hasn't done anything to deserve your love. All she does is cry and demand attention, make messes, and cost you money. But you still love her."

"More than life." She sighed. "That's why I gave her up."

"God loves you even more. And for the same reasons. Because you're His. He made you, even more than you 'made' Alice, because He made you deliberately."

Alaska didn't say anything for a while, and then, there was humor in her tone, but also an underlying sadness when she said, "You're pretty desperate to get me to turn around and drop you off, aren't you? Trying to talk to me about God and all that."

"I told you. You don't have to let me go. Although I would appreciate it if Alice were safe. But I think you want to."

"You're right I do." Without discussing it anymore, she pulled over to the right-hand side of the road as far as she could, then swung around, making a U-turn. The road was pretty much deserted, and it was an easy move to make.

Ellen didn't comment on that, but sat in the passenger seat, praying. Sure that God had put this situation together for the express purpose of drawing Alaska to him, and Ellen just prayed that she didn't mess it up. That she would say whatever it was that God wanted her to say, and that she'd keep her mouth shut around the rest of it.

They must've driven two miles, the blue sky ahead of them, green fields all around them, and the slabs of payment flying by, one after the other, before Alaska spoke again.

"You know, there's a part of me that wants to believe you about God. But I just can't."

"There is a part in every one of us that will never be satisfied until we fill it with God. He created us that way. With a part of us that needs Him. But, the thing about it is, He gives all of us the freedom to choose. We can choose to fill that part with Him, or we can choose to try to fill it with other things that will never make us feel the way God makes us feel. Like we're loved, and that we're complete in him."

"Well I definitely understand what you're talking about, if you're talking about a part of me that never feels satisfied. It's true.

"I have that part too. We all do."

"I don't know about that. I know some people who don't have God, and seem like they're pretty happy."

"Do you think that maybe that's an illusion? Maybe they're faking it? Or maybe, sometimes things seem like they're satisfying us for a while, but they're not. It's like sugar. It tastes good while we're eating it, and we feel full after we're done, but all we did was give ourselves empty calories, and at the same time we took away a little bit of our good health."

Alaska laughed a little, and then she said, "You know, you're pretty persuasive."

"No. It wouldn't matter what I said, if God wants you, He's going to draw you to him no matter who's sitting beside you." Alaska didn't say anything more, and Ellen let everything rest. She didn't want to try to talk Alaska into anything. Talking someone into God was not helpful. They had to make that decision on their own. After all, God could talk them into Himself if He wanted to. It was just her job to show people the way, and let them make the choice for themselves.

"It's that easy?" Alaska said as she slowed down to make the turn to Travis's house. "Just... Tell God you want to be close to Him?"

"Actually, God is so holy, He can't have sin in His presence."

"Well then, that leaves me out. Did you miss the fact that you have the biggest sinner in the world sitting beside you?"

"That's the thing. God knew it. God knew that we would be too big of sinners to ever be able to be in heaven with Him, so He made a way."

"What? Live a pristine life? Being a little goody-goody who goes around taking the sinners' babies and taking care of them?"

"No. It's Jesus. There had to be a payment for the sin. And so God sent his son to pay for us. Once we accept that, our debt is paid in full. And God sees us like Jesus, like there's no sin."

"That's...weird."

"I know. I guess, God created the world, so He can do whatever he wants to. And that's what He did. Knowing that there had to be a payment for the sin - death - and that we couldn't pay that payment, He sent his son to pay for us, and it's that easy."

"It's how easy?" Alaska said, the car slowing down to almost a crawl as she seemed to be thinking about what Ellen had told her.

Ellen didn't feel qualified to continue to talk, she hadn't felt qualified to begin to talk to begin with, but she couldn't stop now.

"We just accept the payment that Jesus made on the cross. The Bible says that we have to repent. We have to understand that we're sinners. Otherwise we wouldn't feel like there needed to be a change and we wouldn't understand that there had to be a payment."

"I know there needs to be a payment. I don't have any problem knowing that I'm a sinner."

"That's part of the reason salvation and God isn't relevant today for most of society. People justify their sin, and refuse to even call it sin. I think maybe Christians have gone along with it to some extent, where we're afraid to tell people that they're sinners. We're afraid to tell them that they're doing something wrong. The world has made that a judgemental thing. And how can people know that they need a Savior if they don't know that they're doing anything wrong?"

"Well I think people know that they're doing things wrong. But, it's easier to pretend that you're not doing anything wrong, if, first of all no one's telling you, and second of all you turn the tables and make them feel like they're wrong if they tell you that you're wrong."

Ellen laughed, knowing that Alaska was exactly right. That was one of the sneaky things the devil had done. He had made it so that it was wrong to tell people that they were sinners. How could they feel like they need a Savior if they didn't know that they were sinners?

"After that, it's easy. God takes everyone. There is no standard. All you have to do is know that you're a sinner and turn from your sin. Because you can't face God and face your sin at the same time. You can't look to Jesus, and still look at your sin. So you have to look away from your sin and look to Jesus. That's called repenting."

"That's something you don't hear much about."

"No. People don't want to admit that there's anything to repent from. They want everything that they do to be okay. But it's not."

"I know."

"And that's it. You have to turn from your sin, turn to Jesus. Confess that you're a sinner, and that you believe Jesus died in payment for your sin. That's the bridge that takes you from being alienated with God, to being a member of God's family. He adopts you. Makes you a child of His, just like Jesus, then when He looks at you, He sees the righteousness of Christ. Because the payment was made, and as far as God is concerned, there is no sin."

"There's no way God can't see my sin." Alaska said, as she pulled into the house, and parked the car, but didn't make any move to shut it off or to get out.

"I could say the same thing. Anyone could. That's so true. But God has given example after example of people in the Bible who were forgiven of sins that we would have thought would be too heinous for anyone to ever forgive. In fact, most of the New Testament was written by a man who persecuted Christians, had them arrested and sent to die, but God turned his life around and he became one of the most influential men in the history of the world after Jesus himself. The Bible makes it clear, God forgives anyone of anything as long as you repent from your sin, turn to Jesus, and trust in Him. God wanted to make it simple so that anyone could do it, even a child. He says that in the Bible too."

"Sounds to me like if you're going to be a Christian you need to know what the Bible says."

"That would probably be my next recommendation. If you're going to be a Christian, you need to read the Bible."

"I think I need to think about this."

"I think you do too. After all, I'd love for you to be a Christian, but it's not up to me to convince you of that. It's up to you to make the choice for yourself."

Alaska nodded, and Ellen prayed as hard as she could that Alaska would make the choice to turn away from her sin, whatever it was, and turn to Jesus. It was a hard choice to make, because a lot of times, change was hard for any reason, but even though they hadn't talked about changing their lifestyle, she could hardly turn from her sin, and turn to Jesus and continue the way she was. It was a change. And changes, even good ones, were scary and hard.

Chapter Twenty

Travis stirred, rolling his head from one side of the pillow to the other before his eyes flew open, and he sat straight up in bed. Alice!

He ripped the covers off and put both feet on the floor before he remembered that Ellen had her.

He sank back down, sitting on the side of the bed, but no longer in a panic.

Ellen. He smiled. She kissed him. Not like a friend.

For a moment he allowed his mind to drift back over all the years. Ellen in the parade. Ellen with her cow and her dog. Ellen with her baby pudge, her little girl face and chubby cheeks, her serious, conscientious, compassionate way. The way she'd been his friend no matter what. The way she'd forgiven him, over and over, for doing stupid things.

The day he'd seen her and realized that what he felt for her was a lot more than the benevolent way an older teenager looks at someone he considers a child. Realizing that he didn't consider Ellen a child any longer. But also realizing that she wasn't ready for the feelings that he had. Making the difficult decision to walk away, rather than do something that both of them would probably regret.

God had rewarded him, over and over, but especially earlier today, when he told her that he loved her and she said she loved him in return. The years of waiting, the years of praying that he was doing the right thing, that God would bring her into his life when she was ready, the uncertainty of whether or not he should continue with Ford, or whether he should be impatient and force things with Ellen. He was glad he had waited, but it hadn't been easy.

And now, all the waiting, all the thinking, all the wishing she was his, was over, and... There were still some hurdles to overcome. Like what they were going to do with Alice.

Like...he should go to Tadgh and ask for her hand. It was an old-fashion gesture, but one that Travis thought should be honored.

Was that rushing things too much? It had been eight years since he first realized that he wanted her. It didn't feel like he was rushing anything to him.

Maybe he should find out exactly how she felt before he embarrassed himself by going to her father, but it seemed like that was backwards. He ought to find out whether or not Tadgh would give him permission, before he pursued anything more with Ellen. He'd already kissed her. He probably shouldn't have even done that.

Knowing that the world would think he was nuts. Knowing that they would laugh at the idea that a woman's father should be consulted, and that she shouldn't make up her own mind, Travis didn't care. It was a matter of respecting the man who had raised Ellen, and giving him the honor that was his due. He wasn't asking for Tadgh to hand Ellen to him, just asking for permission, to see if Tadgh felt like he was good enough to pursue after the woman he'd raised.

At that thought, his stomach churned. Maybe Tadgh really wouldn't think he was good enough. After all, his beginnings were less than humble. They were despicable. His family didn't exactly have the track record of being faithful and honorable. If he were Tadgh... Just looking at him from the outside, he wasn't sure whether he would give himself permission to pursue Ellen.

He thought he heard a vehicle, and he smiled, but no knock at the door was forthcoming, nor did he hear the front door open or Ellen call out.

That was odd.

He stood up, walking to the window looking out, seeing a little bit of dust like maybe there had been a vehicle, and he tried to remember if he had ordered anything where there might've been a delivery person at his house, but he hadn't.

Strange.

He shook his head, and moved away from the window, getting ready for his day. Thinking to himself that maybe he needed to make a phone call to Tadgh before he did anything else, he called Tadgh and arranged a time for him to come out and talk.

He had made a lot of calls for business over the years, a lot of difficult calls, a lot of ones he didn't want to make, or ones that had intimidated him. But, the call to Tadgh was by far the hardest call he'd ever made.

He dreaded the idea of facing the man, not because he wasn't a good man or didn't like him, but because he was so emotionally invested in the outcome and did not want to go see him.

But, for Ellen, he would do it.

He went down to the kitchen and had cracked a couple of eggs when he heard a vehicle. This time, he stopped what he was doing and walked to the window in time to see Ellen's car coming down the driveway. He smiled before he realized that...it wasn't Ellen driving.

He squinted, were those tattoos?

His eyes moved, and he realized that it was Ellen's honey blonde hair in the passenger seat.

A slither of unease curled through his stomach, and he threw the egg shell that he had still held in his hand in the garbage can before he walked to the back door.

It took a couple of seconds watching Ellen's car pull in and stop, before he realized there was movement on the stoop.

It took even longer for him to process what he saw.

A small child, young, sat at his feet on the stoop. He seemed agitated as he moved his legs from side to side, and his fingers clenched and unclenched. It was almost like he was forcing himself to keep his butt on the stoop, but his body just had to move.

Strange. Travis looked around. There were no adults in sight.

Ellen had gotten out of her car. The driver's door opened a few seconds later, and he recognized, almost immediately, Alice's mother.

What in the world was she doing here? And why was she driving Ellen's car?

Still, despite all the things that seem to be really odd about the day, he could smile, because he remembered how his day had started. With Ellen, holding her. It wasn't hard to remember the way she kissed him, and how perfect she felt in his arms.

He opened the door, as Ellen pulled Alice from the backseat and closed the door.

She smiled at him, but as her eyes fell to the bottom step, and she realized there was a child sitting on it, her smile faded. And her brows drew down, as though trying to figure out this newest development.

As he was. He had stepped out on the porch, and slowly made his way down the steps.

He wasn't very good with small children, and in his experience, a lot of times they were afraid of him.

He didn't want to scare this little guy off. Not before he figured out what in the world was going on. He was way too young to be anywhere without supervision. There was a small bag sitting beside the kid, and Travis made it to the step, hunching down beside the bag, as Ellen walked up the sidewalk.

The kid's eyes were on the women, and he jumped a little at Travis's voice.

"Hey there, Mister," Travis said, using the most gentle voice he could muster up.

"Hey," the kid said.

"Where's your mom?" Travis asked.

The kid's eyes skittered from Travis to Ellen and back to Travis.

"The man told me to sit here. That you took in kids, and that you'd take me."

Travis's eyes grew wide. He took in kids?

He almost laughed. Not voluntarily. Not because he wanted to. Just because he hadn't had a choice, but...he supposed word got around. Especially in the circles that this kid's parents must run in.

"Is he coming back for you?" he asked.

He regretted that question immediately as the child's chin trembled, and his eyes fell. Instead of answering, he picked up an envelope that was lying on the other side of him, which Travis hadn't noticed until just then, and shoved it at Travis.

Travis assumed the answer was in the envelope, but he wasn't sure. He lifted eyes full of questions to Ellen's. She hadn't said a word, just stood there, holding the car seat and waiting. Listening.

He didn't know what else to do, so he opened the envelope and pulled out a piece of paper and read the note.

> Hi!
>
> This is Eugene. Travis Feagley is his dad, and while I raised him for the first four years of his life, I can no longer take care of him, so I brought him to his father's house, so his dad can start pulling his weight.
>
> Now that Travis is successful, he can start paying for his own child.
>
> I'll be back around to check on him. He's not ready for school yet, but I'll make sure that Travis has parental consent and all the records that he needs when I come back.
>
> Signed,
> Eugene's mom.

Chapter Twenty-One

Ellen stood on the steps and stared at Travis. He smiled at her, but then, as he read the note, his smile had faded and something that looked suspiciously like panic took over his features.

He seemed to have gotten himself a little bit together when he lifted his eyes.

"I thought I heard a vehicle earlier. But I didn't see it. I didn't realize he was sitting here until I looked out the window and saw you, and came to the door to greet you."

She nodded. He didn't seem to be done, and so she didn't say anything. She felt, rather than saw, Alaska come up behind her, and stand just to her side.

"This letter says that I'm his father. I promise you, it's not true."

She stared at him. This was the second child that had been dropped off at his house. But Travis was supposed to be the father of this one.

She felt something hard form in her stomach. It was heavy and hurt.

"It says you're the dad?"

"I'm telling you, it's not true."

She believed him. She had to. She didn't even need to look down at the child, see his bright blue eyes, and blonde hair, and know he didn't look anything like Travis, to believe that the kid wasn't his.

Travis had been faithful. He said he had, and he didn't lie. Ever.

"I believe you," she said simply.

He closed his eyes, as the breath blew out of him.

It surprised her that he'd been worried that she might not believe him. But that's what it looked like.

"Ellen, I promise you it's not true," he said again, standing and coming down the stairs.

He didn't stop until his arms were around her, and he took the car carrier from her hands, as he pulled her close.

"I believe you," she said simply, and again.

"If you're not the dad, why did the letter say you were?" Alaska asked, and while Ellen wanted to pull closer, lift her head and touch her lips to Travis's, she pulled back instead.

"Why did you say that the father of your baby was Roger, when it wasn't?"

Alaska didn't need to say anything more. It was funny that she'd even asked to begin with, since she'd done the exact same thing. Obviously she did it to force Travis to take the child. Because she wanted something better for her child than what she could provide for it.

"You've met Alice's mom, her name is Alaska," Ellen said, as she put an arm around Travis's waist, and he put his arm around her shoulders, pulling her close to him. She loved the way he felt, solid and strong beside her.

"Good to meet you," Travis said, but his words sounded guarded, like he was waiting for the other shoe to drop.

She couldn't blame him, since it seemed like he'd had a lot of things dropping in his life lately.

"Is the man coming back?" a little voice asked, one that trembled, and sounded like it was close to tears.

"His name's Eugene," Travis said.

Ellen dropped to her knees. "Hi Eugene. I'm Ellen."

"I'm scared," Eugene said, and he stopped trying not to cry.

All three adults froze for an instant. Before Ellen could reach out to Eugene, Alaska had wrapped her arms around the little boy.

He didn't necessarily come willingly; he wanted his mom. But, he allowed her to take him, and fold him into her embrace.

Ellen watched, her heart cracking. Alaska had so many issues of her own. They hadn't even gotten into those in the car, but just counting the ones Ellen knew about. Whatever caused her to give up her own baby to begin with. Maybe that was what made her reach out for Eugene. Because she could relate to a mom who felt like they couldn't take care of their child.

She bit her lips, and looked at Travis. He had an expression on his face that she couldn't read. It was a little bit of tenderness, maybe a little frustration too. And she could understand that. It felt like sin messed everything up. It was frustrating when people made bad choices, and children suffered because of it.

"I need to go back to the farm. I haven't fed my cows today, and I need to take care of my dogs as well." She spoke quietly to Travis and he nodded.

"Do you mind if I come along?"

"I'd love it."

Eugene was still crying, but his cries weren't quite as loud as they had been when he started out.

"Ellen and I are going to head out for a bit." Travis spoke. Alaska's head came up, and she nodded as she looked at him, never letting go of the little boy who clung to her now. "I'll take the kids...or at least take Eugene if you want to spend some time with Alice."

"I'll keep them both." Alaska's voice held determination.

Ellen and Travis looked at each other. She could keep Alice for sure; the baby was hers. And she didn't seem to want to let go of Eugene. Travis lifted her brows, as though asking her if it was okay with her to leave them with Alaska. She shrugged and nodded.

"I cracked some eggs, and they're on the counter. If you want to cook them, you're welcome to. There's bacon in the fridge."

He hadn't walked away from the carseat, and Ellen could see his struggle as he looked down at the baby. He had fallen head over heels in love with her, and having Alaska come back was going to be hard for him. Especially if she wanted her child back. But how could they not let her go?

Ellen almost laughed because her concern had been for Travis, but the idea of Alice being taken away was almost more than she could handle. She loved the baby, too.

"I'll be here when you get back," Alaska said, and her chin came up. Ellen recognized that look easily. It was a look of someone who was going to keep going, even though they felt like quitting.

"Alice is probably going to be hungry soon," Ellen offered. "I had her for two hours and she hasn't eaten the whole time." Ellen looked down at the baby whose big eyes were blinking as she stared out at the adults surrounding her.

She wiggled a bit, as her hands moved jerkily in front of her face.

Ellen's heart squeezed. She was so precious.

Precious life, created in the image of God, who needed a mom and a dad to love her and raise her and provide a stable home for her, a place of refuge, a place where she learned all that she needed to know in order to move through life. To handle what life held out for her, to handle what life threw at her.

Alaska stood, holding Eugene in her arms.

"I can carry the baby in for you," Travis said, his face unsmiling.

Ellen didn't have a problem reading what was on it. He was reluctant, but resigned. Alaska nodded, and Ellen waited while he disappeared into the house. She was reluctant, yet resigned as well. And even though she knew that if Alaska came back and wanted her baby, it was for the best, it still hurt.

She could only imagine what it was doing to Travis. He had been on board from the beginning, had risen to the challenge without complaint. Ellen had helped, but she hadn't thought from the beginning that the baby was going to be hers. At first she thought she was going to be finding a nanny for it.

That hadn't happened.

And she assumed, after what had transpired between Travis and her, that...that wouldn't be necessary? She wasn't sure. Maybe they should talk about it. She didn't know how quickly he was going to want to move. As for her, she felt like she'd been waiting forever, and wanted to take the next step immediately. But, that didn't necessarily adhere to the world's idea of wisdom, and she knew Travis would rather do things right than do things fast. After all, it had taken him eight years to finally tell her that he loved her.

Then too, there was also the fact that Travis could relate to being abandoned and neglected as a child. That would affect the way he treated the children that had landed at his doorstep, but it might also affect the way they moved in their relationship. It might be hard for him to trust that she wouldn't leave him. That she meant what she said when she said she loved him.

Of course, he might also be concerned that she didn't really believe that the child wasn't his. After all, if the note declared that he was the dad, most people would believe it.

"Are you ready?" he said as he came out the door. His voice was heavy with sorrow and concern.

"I think it will do us good to get away. Were you able to get some rest?"

He nodded. "I woke up in a panic, because I forgot that you had taken the baby."

"I'm sorry."

"No. It's fine. I'm glad. But, you know how you're in a deep sleep and all of the sudden you think you might've missed something that you were supposed to be responsible for."

"Yeah." They went down the steps together, Chewy at her heels and as they walked the short distance to his truck, he took her hand.

Their fingers slid together, and he squeezed. She looked up, and he was looking down at her, a serious expression on his face.

"I've wanted to do that for a long time," he said simply.

She knew exactly what he was saying. She probably wanted it for just as long, if not longer. After all, she was crushing on him when he was crushing on Shanna.

Thinking of Shanna made her eyes rove over his face. Most of the bruises had disappeared, the scab had fallen off. There was a small scar where his face had been cut, but she bet that it would heal over eventually. His stubble mostly hid it, anyway.

"You healed up well."

"I'm baring my heart to her, and all she can think of is the guy who hit me."

She smiled, knowing he was teasing her. "I was thinking of your face, not of Chalmer. I actually haven't seen him since that night."

"Me, either. But I have a feeling I'll be seeing him again. Maybe in some back alley some dark night he thinks he can get a jump on me."

She was silent. That sounded like something Chalmer would do. It made her a little scared for him. She didn't believe in going around, living life with fear, but she also believed that it was wise to take precautions and being careful.

"I can see that happening. I...hope you are careful."

"Of course." He gave her a grin that said that his idea of being careful was probably not the same as hers.

But she wasn't going to give him a hard time about it. There really wasn't a whole lot she could say beyond that, and he most likely wasn't going to listen to her anymore than what he already did.

"I called your uncle this morning."

"Oh?" she said, as he walked to her side of the truck, and opened the door for her.

It was an unexpected courtesy which made her smile, as she lifted her face to his.

"Thank you," she said, her hand on the door, although there was something on his face that made her stop.

"My pleasure," he said. His words sounded distracted.

They stood there for a moment, before he murmured, "I guess I didn't get to kiss you good morning. I spent a lot of time thinking about our last kiss. It was...better than all the ones I had dreamed about."

Her fingertips tingled, and her toes curled. Just the idea that he dreamed about kissing her. Not like she hadn't spent more time dreaming about his kiss.

"Same," she said, rather than arguing about who had spent more time thinking about kissing who. "Maybe I need another one to compare it to. Just in case I'm remembering wrong," she said, knowing it was a flimsy excuse, but wanting him to kiss her again.

"If you want me to kiss you, you should just say, 'Travis, kiss me please.' It's not like it would be a hardship."

"Travis, kiss me please." She couldn't help smiling, as her hand landed on his chest, and she leaned forward.

"I was just thinking that I shouldn't kiss you again until I've gotten your uncle's permission. I'm a little nervous."

"My uncle's permission to kiss me?" she said, backing up just a bit. That was interesting.

"You know. When the man asks the father for permission to marry his daughter."

"You want to get married?" she breathed out, her words barely making a sound.

"Is that crazy?"

"...I guess not. It's what I want, but... I thought it might take you a while to come around to that, since it took you eight years to get around to telling me that you loved me."

"You were too young. I wanted to tell you a long time ago." He seemed concerned that she might have thought that he delayed on purpose. Or delayed because he wasn't sure.

"Why are you nervous? You know my uncle loves you. He thinks you're amazing."

"Really? He knows what I was. He knows where I came from. He might not think I'm good enough for you. I don't think I'm good enough for you."

"I think where you came from makes it even more amazing to see where you are now. And, my uncle might not agree, but I feel like I'm not good enough for you. You have become successful, you've traveled the world, you've amassed a lot of business skills and ability and you've invested in our town. I'm still a small time farmer, with my cows and my dogs and not much else."

"Maybe that doesn't look successful in the eyes of the world, but you've been a faithful friend. That's worth more than all the money in the world. I ought to know. If it were possible to buy friendship, I could afford to."

She didn't say anything, because he was right. Friendship was something that couldn't be bought. Loyalty, trust, and support. She couldn't pay a person to do that; they had to do it of their own free will.

"Are you telling me that I just asked you to kiss me, because you told me to. And now you're not going to because you're waiting for Uncle Tadgh to give permission?"

The serious look of his face was marred a little as his lips curved up. "That doesn't seem like a very nice thing to do, doesn't it?"

"No, it doesn't," she said, affecting a bit of a hurt tone.

"Then I guess you have to kiss me. That way if anyone asks, I can say that I was blindsided, you wrapped your arms around me and kissed me before I could know what was happening." His smile turned up even more. "Of course, if I end up pulling you closer, and kissing you back, I guess there's really no excuse for that, is there?"

"Maybe we'll just have to see if you can resist my charms," she said, blinking her eyes and realizing she was flirting.

"I can't say that I'm going to put too much effort into that," Travis murmured as she came closer, and he lowered his head so she could reach.

Their lips met, and she realized she had been remembering the first kiss incorrectly. Or perhaps, they'd gotten better with practice, since the second kiss was far, far better.

Chapter Twenty-Two

Travis found himself humming as they pulled into the driveway going toward Ellen's house. It was just over the hill from his, but to drive there meant going out his driveway, going down the road a half a mile, then pulling into Ellen's driveway.

It wasn't enough time for him to lose the glow that he felt after Ellen had gotten done kissing him. It definitely wasn't him that had gotten done. He had been ready to stand there all day, but one of them had pulled back. He was pretty sure it was her. He was a little cloudy on the details, because kissing Ellen seemed to do that to his brain. Turning it to mush, making it so that all he could do was want her closer.

Still, as her house came into sight, and he saw her uncle walking across the yard from the barn toward the house, his stomach tightened. Ellen seemed confident that her uncle would be fine with them, but he wasn't so sure. After all, just the little bit of time that he'd spent with Alice made him realize how much a man could feel protective toward a baby in his care. If he felt that way toward Alice, whom he had only known for a couple of weeks, he could only imagine the way Tadgh must feel about Ellen.

Travis had a hard time picturing anyone being good enough for Alice. That had to be the way Tadgh felt too.

"You can let me off at the barn," Ellen said, and he noticed her lips were still a little swollen. Maybe he'd been a little too rough and hadn't realized it. But she didn't seem to be complaining. He'd have to keep that in mind.

"That way you and Uncle Tadgh can have some privacy for your talk."

"You're leaving me to the wolves by myself?"

"I have confidence in you," she said, with a saucy tilt to her head, as he pulled to a stop and she hopped out, making Chewy stay on the seat.

He wanted to kiss her goodbye, but that seemed a little silly, since he just gotten done kissing her a couple of minutes before.

She waved as she crossed in front of the truck. Chewy whined, but stayed beside him.

He watched her smile at him before she headed toward the barn.

As he turned back toward the house, he saw that Tadgh had stopped, and watched as he came closer.

Travis took a deep breath, knowing that what he said in the next few minutes, and what was said to him, could affect the rest of his life. He wanted to do his best.

Parking his truck, he said a short prayer, and then got out, slamming the door shut and walking over to where Tadgh waited.

He held out his hand. "Hey there," he said.

Tadgh shook his hand, looking him dead in the eye. "I wondered when I was going to get a call like that. Or even if I was."

"It seemed like the right thing to do. I've been taking care of Alice now for a couple of weeks, and it's given me a new perspective about how a man might feel towards a child he's raised."

"Gets worse over time," Tadgh said. "Take a walk behind the house?" He jerked his head indicating the path around the house.

They started out, with Travis trying to think of how best to start the conversation.

They stopped at the back porch, where Tadgh invited him to sit down. Travis didn't want to be rude, but he didn't think he could sit right now.

"No sir, if it's okay I'd rather stand. I'm a little nervous." He'd found in business that it was often good to admit the truth. Even if the person felt like it would make them seem weaker in everyone else's eyes. He could project confidence while admitting that he wasn't totally confident. People seem to relate to weakness, as long as it didn't seem to be a weakness that a person couldn't overcome.

That was just his experience. It seemed to work with Tadgh, because he smiled. But there was still concern in his eyes.

"You're nervous. That makes me nervous. What's up?"

"I guess you've known that I've been away for a while."

"Yeah," Tadgh said. If he thought what Travis said was ridiculous, his face didn't show it.

Everyone in town knew he'd been gone, so Travis knew he should have opened slightly differently. But it was done now.

"Ford Hansen wanted me to, and I appreciated it. But there was another reason I left."

"Okay."

"I was in love with Ellen."

Tadgh's face remained impassive. The only thing that gave away his surprise was two blinks.

He slowly nodded, and then he said, "Okay." The way he said it seemed to be an invitation for Travis to continue speaking.

"She was only fourteen. I was eighteen. That would have been a relationship that was inappropriate. So I had to go."

"I see."

"Yeah. It was one of the hardest things I've done, but I loved Ellen, and I wanted the best for her."

"I think you made the right choice."

"I know I did. I wanted to come back when she was eighteen, that was my plan. But Ford sent me to Brazil. Maybe he did that on purpose because he wanted Ellen to have a little bit more time to grow. I don't know."

"Knowing Ford, that's certainly possible," Tadgh agreed.

Travis paused, and took a breath. He couldn't tell anything by looking at Tadgh's face. Not about what he was thinking, not about what he was going to say. So he plunged ahead. Feeling more nervous then he would have if he were brokering a multimillion dollar business deal.

"I promise you. I never touched her. I wanted to," and his fingers tightened at the memory. He clenched them into fists in his pocket. "I really did. But, it wouldn't have been right." He wanted credit for that. But maybe that didn't mean anything to Tadgh, or maybe Tadgh expected it, and would have accepted no less. Regardless, it hadn't been the way Travis had been raised to act, and walking away from Ellen had been the most difficult thing he'd ever done. "We were friends. She wrote to me. I'm sure you probably knew that."

"I did."

"We talked on the phone occasionally, but I never told her how I felt. I never knew how she felt. Just that she agreed to be my friend, and that had to be enough until the time came for more."

"I see."

"I'm back to stay. Back in Sweet Water. I know that if you look at me, look at where I came from, look at my parents, my mom, if you use that to judge what kind of man I might be, you wouldn't think that I was going to amount to much." Tadgh's lips stayed pressed close, but he lifted his chin acknowledging Travis's words.

"But I think I've used that to learn. To teach myself what I didn't want to be. To try to pick up traits that are opposite from what I was raised with."

Tadgh didn't say anything, Travis wasn't sure whether he should stay silent for a bit, and see if the man had something to say, or just finish what had turned out to be quite a speech. Considering he hadn't planned on talking long at all. But he felt like he needed to make his case. Felt like he needed to have some kind of argument in favor of himself. But he had to be honest too.

"The last few weeks as I've been taking care of Alice, I realized that... I don't think I'll ever look at a boy and think that he was good enough for my daughter. Certainly I wouldn't think that anyone would look at me and think that I was good enough. The only thing I can say is, God loves me. And I'm going to do my best to please Him. And I'd like to do that with Ellen beside me. Sir, I'm asking for your permission to spend time with your daughter with the intention of marrying her if she'll have me."

He held his breath, meeting Tadgh's eyes, and waiting. Every second that ticked by felt like an eternity was tucked inside.

A bird chirped and fluttered in the bush beside the house, while another one flapped overhead and the wind stirred the grass, making a swishing sound that wasn't nearly loud enough to drown out the beating of his heart.

Say something.

"I'd heard that you had a baby dropped off. Probably like the rest of the state. A town like Sweet Water can be depended on to spread gossip the way small towns do."

A ghost of a smile crossed Tadgh's face, before he became serious once more.

"You're right about where you came from. But you're family, too. Ford and I spent more than one evening discussing how we could help. We would often say to each other that you can offer to help, but if you reach out a hand, the person you're trying to help needs to reach up and clasp it back. You've certainly done that."

Travis swallowed. This didn't feel good.

"You're right about how protective I feel toward Ellen too. Her father was my brother, and I loved her. I promised I would do my best to raise Ellen. She practically raised herself. But I do feel protective of her. And I can't help but be a little proud of the woman she's become. Maybe not successful in the world's eyes, but I do believe God will tell her 'well done thou good and faithful servant,' and that's what she should be living for anyway."

"I agree."

Tadgh simply jerked his head in acknowledgment of Travis's words and continued speaking.

"I didn't know you loved her back when you guys were so young. I would have...tried harder to keep you apart. I figured she was young, and you were a little more versed in the ways of the world, plus I thought you had your eyes on a cheerleader at school."

"She blinded me for a bit." He couldn't deny it.

"But there was no substance there. I think you figured that out."

"I did."

"That's good, because some men never do. Some men are always drawn to fool's gold, and never understand that there is no value there."

Travis didn't say anything. He might have been fooled at one time. He probably could still be fooled again, but not by that. Not by someone who didn't have the heart that Ellen did. The compassion, the character. The loyalty. That was probably what got him more than anything. She had stuck with him, no matter what he had done. He loved that, and at the same time, he knew he owed her, because he hadn't been as loyal. Not at first anyway.

"Ford kept me informed of your progress, the things you've done, and you probably don't know about that."

"No. I didn't."

"It's been nothing but glowing reports of you. He's pleased beyond words with what you've done with the opportunities that you've been given. But more than that, he extols your character, your honesty, your integrity, and the compassion you have toward others. I might have been concerned that after having a baby dumped on your doorstep, you were only interested in Ellen so that you would have cheap labor, a nanny to take care of your responsibility."

Travis opened his mouth to protest. He didn't want Tadgh to think that the baby was actually his. He also didn't want Tadgh to think that he only wanted Ellen because of what she could give him. But he also wanted to be as honest as he could, and he wondered if he should mention the little boy that had been dropped off that morning. If Tadgh had heard the rumors about the baby, he would certainly hear the rumors about the little boy as well. But Tadgh held up his hand, stopping any protest.

"I know that's not the way it's been. I didn't really need you to tell me that you've been in love with her for the last eight years, in order to know that you aren't just looking at her as a meal ticket."

"No. Never." He almost laughed. He had plenty of money. He could afford to hire ten nannies if he wanted to.

"Because Ellen would work herself into the ground for you. I'm sure you know that."

"Yes, sir. I do."

"But I have the feeling that you would do the same for her. If I didn't think that, it would be a lot harder for me to give my consent. But, I think you're a man who will take care of her. But not just that, I believe you will cherish her the way she's meant to be cherished. You have my permission to court my daughter."

Just like that.

Travis had to stand there for a minute. He thought he was going to have to get into the fact that he had two children that weren't really his, but that were his responsibility, and Ellen was probably going to be helping him with them, and that he was going to have to try to convince Tadgh that neither one of them were actually his. That he really had been faithful to Ellen. But Tadgh hadn't even questioned the fact that he was faithful. He just assumed it.

Gratefulness that Tadgh had looked at his character, and not at his family or at the rumors of the town, but had instead, seen the best in him, welled up inside of him, closing off his throat. To the point where he could barely talk.

"Thank you sir. I don't believe that one person can make another person happy, but I do believe that I can create an atmosphere where she can thrive, and I know for a fact that I can love her better than any other person in the world. I'll spend the rest of my life proving that."

"I believe you will, son." Tadgh's eyes were serious. His look intense. "You're getting the very best girl I know. But I do believe that I'm getting the best son-in-law I possibly could. I'd love to have you be part of our family." Tadgh held out his hand.

Travis stared at it for what felt like a very long moment. All of his life he hadn't felt like he belonged anywhere. He longed for a dad, someone to teach them how to be a man. He longed for his mother to love him, and he never felt accepted by her, or wanted for that matter. And here was this man, looking at him and seeing the best, allowing him to have his daughter, and telling him he would love to have him be part of his family.

It was almost too much.

He took his hand, shook it, and said, "Thank you." The words just didn't seem adequate, but he couldn't say anything more.

Maybe Tadgh understood that, or maybe it was just how he was, but instead of letting go of his hand, he pulled on it, pulling Travis to him, putting first one arm around him and slapping him on the back and then pulling him close in a bearhug. Which Travis returned. He appreciated this man, and knew it was only because of Ellen that he was in his life.

He had so much to be grateful for, grateful to the Lord for all of the opportunities, to Ford for caring about him, but most of all, for Ellen.

There were times over the years where he was lonely, alone, and where he might have been tempted to try to find someone else. He never had, and he did not regret being faithful. Not one bit. Especially at that moment, he was thankful that he had determined in his heart from the very beginning to be faithful. Things could have been a lot different if he hadn't.

As Tadgh's grip loosened, and they stepped back, he thought maybe Tadgh wiped a tear from his eye, but couldn't say for sure. He clamped a hand on his shoulder and said, "Come on. Did Ellen know what you were asking me?"

"I told her I didn't think I should kiss her until I'd asked your permission."

"Have you kissed her?" Tadgh asked, as he stepped down off the porch.

He wanted to lie, but he couldn't. That would be wrong. Plus, eventually Tadgh would figure out the truth, and he would think even less of Travis for not being able to tell the truth to begin with.

"Twice. The second time was better than the first."

Tadgh laughed.

"It's the practice, and that's the way a good relationship is. I know every time I kiss my wife, it gets better. She claims it's because we've practiced more, but I just think that's the way it is when two people love each other. The relationship gets sweeter as long as you continue to put the effort in that it takes."

"I don't know how much effort it's going to take, but I'm willing to do whatever I need to. After my relationship with the Lord, Ellen is the most important thing in the world to me."

"I actually believe that son. And I think you will. You can spend a lifetime trying to be the best husband possible, and you'll never reach the end of your potential. Speaking from experience."

Chapter Twenty-Three

Ellen stood with Daisy, scratching her ears. Daisy had been one of the foundation cows of her herd of almost fifty Highland cows. It was hard to believe she'd been raising them for over ten years.

Still, it was spring, and there wasn't much to do regarding feeding them. They were on pasture, and all of them had calved earlier in the year. The calves were tagged and banded and it wasn't yet time to give them their vaccines or worm them.

So she checked her water trough, and then walked around the herd, looking at the babies. She didn't have her dogs with her. When they saw cows, they wanted to work. Even Chewy, who was her best trained canine, would be trembling with excitement at the idea of getting to do her job.

It amazed Ellen sometimes how much the dogs just loved doing what they were bred to do.

Regardless, she stopped by Daisy, and had stood scratching her for a while. Wondering what the men were talking about.

She knew that her uncle loved Travis, and she didn't think that he would have any problem at all giving Travis permission. Her uncle could be a little bit unique, and she could see him giving Travis parameters, like he had to wait for a year, or some such other nonsense.

Ellen hoped not. She wanted to get married right away. She'd been waiting forever, and she didn't want to keep waiting. She wanted to get that part of her life started.

She knew all the wisdom, that she should enjoy her independence while she had it and all that, but she felt like that was the world's wisdom. She didn't see that anywhere in the Bible. Other than Paul saying that he could serve God better if a man didn't have a wife and kids.

Actually, she felt like the world's wisdom went against what the Bible said. Because a person wasn't supposed to enjoy their independence. They were supposed to find a mate and raise children in the nurture and admonition of the Lord. A woman was supposed to keep her house. It didn't say anything about fulfilling herself, or having independence, or enjoying time before she was tied down. None of those things were biblical.

Maybe the reason people struggled in marriage was because they were taught to indulge themselves, rather than being brought up to serve others, with a focus on learning to make a godly home and raise children that loved the Lord.

Ellen laughed at herself a bit. She might be singing a different tune ten years from now, although the Bible wouldn't be. It would still be saying the exact same thing. But she did know that a person had a tendency to think they knew a lot until they actually got into whatever it was they thought they knew a lot about, and then they realized they didn't know quite as much as what they thought they did.

"You look pretty good for a ten-year-old," she said to Daisy, scratching down her backbone.

She didn't want to think about how time slipped by, and eventually it would be time for Daisy to move on. That was part of farming, but it wasn't a part that Ellen relished. It would be nice to have Travis beside her when those hard decisions had to be made. She'd have someone to hold her hand and dry her tears.

Of course, men weren't exactly known for their compassion. Maybe Travis wouldn't want to put his arm around her and comfort her.

She tried to think about that, whether he would be that kind of husband or not.

Did it matter?

She hadn't figured that out, when she looked up to see him walking across the field, a big smile on his face.

She didn't have to ask whether or not Tadgh said yes. Of course, she hadn't been worried about that at all.

She left Daisy, and started walking toward him, her steps much faster than usual.

By the time they met, they were both walking as fast as they could, and maybe she even took a few running steps as he lifted her up in his arms, and swung her around.

She laughed, holding on to him, as the world spun crazily around her.

He kissed her before he even set her down, and she was fine with that. She didn't need to talk about it at all. He pulled away, before allowing her to slide down so her feet were on the ground, but he kept her pressed close to him.

"I guess you can tell he said yes."

"I was getting that impression," she said, a little breathless, still holding on to him to help keep her balance.

"I didn't realize he liked me that much."

"You don't give yourself nearly enough credit," she said, and while she was smiling, she meant it. He still thought of himself as the boy with the mother who was addicted to drugs, who would leave her children at home by themselves while she went and slept with a man for money in order to buy her next fix.

She didn't know whether Travis would ever come out from under that cloud, but she had to admit she loved that he stayed humble. That he didn't think of himself as some big shot, even though he had gone away and become successful.

"Well, credit or no, I have his blessing to ask you to marry me."

"What are you waiting for?" she asked, only partially teasing. Part of her was afraid that the other shoe was going to drop and she was going to find out that they had to wait five years or something.

"I want to do it right. I don't even have a ring yet. I mean, I thought about getting one, but I wasn't sure whether I should take you with me, so we could pick it out together, or if I should get one on my own. I...

You don't wear a whole lot of jewelry and I don't have any idea of what you like."

"Something small and unpretentious." That was easy. She didn't wear a lot of jewelry, because she wasn't a bling bling kind of person.

"See? I would've wanted to get you the biggest rock I could find, so the whole world knows that you're mine."

"Well you can do that if you want to. It might get in the way when I'm trying to feed my cows though."

He laughed. "And that's what I love about you."

"That's all you love about me?" she teased.

"I don't know. There might be something else in there."

"Well, I love how quick you are to ask a girl to marry you. Hint hint."

"Really? I wanted to spend the next year courting you. You deserve that much. You know, candlelight dinners, date nights, trips to The Cities and just spending fun time together without any responsibilities."

"First of all, I don't deserve anything. And secondly, I don't care about any of that. I just want to be with you."

"Really?" he asked, and his tone had turned tender. Maybe there was a little wonder in it, like he couldn't believe that she could look at him and see someone that she wanted to spend so much time with.

"Really. Do I have to ask you?" She put a hand on her hip, and leaned back a little, looking up into his face and trying to put a stern look on hers.

"You can if you want to. I'm not going to turn you down."

"Kind of want to. But I don't want that to be the precedent for our marriage. I don't want to run ahead of you, and I suppose if you're going to be the head of our household, I ought to get used to relaxing, and making sure that I'm doing my job. The job God gave me. And not trying to do your job too. After all, if He thought I could do two jobs, He would have given them both to me."

"You know, sometimes I think about that. How much pressure that puts on me. A man in general I guess. After all, I answer to God for what I do. How I treat you, how I run our household. The decisions I make He is watching, and He wants to make sure I treat you right."

"That's funny, because I think a lot of men think that God put them in charge, so they can boss their wife around, make her a servant, while they get to do whatever they want, and the wife has to submit. But I think the way you see it is the way it's supposed to be. After all, just because you're the husband doesn't mean that you get to not be a Christian anymore, and as a Christian, we're supposed to serve others."

She didn't feel it was her place to lecture him on what the Bible commanded him to do, but he seemed to know. Maybe it was something that he'd been thinking about. Maybe he had used those extra years to study what the Bible said about what a husband was supposed to do. How he was supposed to treat his wife, and think about what kind of husband God wanted him to be.

"Exactly. The Bible says I'm supposed to love you the way I love myself. I kind of think that's funny, since the Bible doesn't have to command us to love ourselves. No one deliberately is unkind or draconian to themselves. Why would I be that way to my wife?" He brushed a hand down her cheek, and she put hers over top of it, pressing it against her skin. "I think remembering that you are a child of God, and I don't want to get to heaven and explain to God why I wasn't kind to His daughter."

"I couldn't imagine you being unkind. Couldn't imagine you being anything but the best husband you can be."

"I'm not going to be perfect," he warned her.

"I know. And, I'm unlikely to be perfect either." She wondered if those words would come back to haunt her. How many meals she would burn, or forget to cook altogether. Sometimes she did that already, where she got so involved in something that she forgot it was time to eat, and it was particularly discouraging when Ashley had been counting on her to make supper. Most of the time Ashley laughed and said she'd done the same thing. She hoped Travis would be as forgiving.

She wasn't really worried about it. Travis had never had a temper, and because he was so humble, she hardly thought that he would hold her to a higher standard than what he had for himself.

Of course, it didn't matter what he did. The Bible had commands for her, and it didn't command her to make sure that he did what he was supposed to. She was just supposed to make sure she did what she was supposed to. And let God handle everything else.

"Were you serious about not wanting to be courted? To just get married?" he asked, both of his hands sliding down as he gripped hers between them.

She squeezed. "Yes. Completely serious."

"I don't even have a place to live."

"What's wrong with the house you're living in?"

"It's not exactly the kind of place where I wanted to bring my bride."

"We can wait if you want to. But I don't need a fancy house."

"I don't have a place for your cows."

"We can ask Tadgh if he'll keep them until we have a place."

She didn't mean to rebut every one of his arguments, but what he was concerned about did not bother her at all.

"I just don't want you to not like what we do. If it's more important for you to have everything perfect, and to wait, then I'll suck it up." She gave a brief smile. Only half joking.

He stared down at her, serious, his thumbs brushing over the backs of her fingers softly, like he didn't even realize what he was doing.

Finally, he lowered onto one knee, and looked up into her face.

"I wanted more for you. Truly. But, we did wait a really long time. Almost a decade. The idea that you don't care to wait until I get everything set up perfectly I think is a little more temptation than what I can handle. I want to be with you for the rest of my life, and I wanted to start as soon as possible. Eight years is long enough to wait. Will you marry me?"

She smiled, she couldn't help herself, and she nodded her head, before she could clear her throat and say, "Yes. Yes."

There weren't any other words, and thankfully he didn't seem to need them, as he stood back up, the glow on his face surely matching hers, as he grabbed her and held her close, pulling her against him and kissing her, a different kind of kiss than before. It was full of promises and hopes and dreams and the passion of eight long years of waiting.

"How soon?" He lifted his head after a while and breathed into her ear.

"Today?" she said, just as breathless and just as soft.

He laughed. "I love you."

"I love you too." Forever. All of her life. Until she died. She would love this man.

She wanted to tell him all of that and more, but his phone started to ring, startling them, and she looked around, trying to figure out where the sound came from.

"What a time for a phone call."

"It's probably best. We ought to get back anyway. We have plans to make. And, who knows what's going on with the children."

"It's Alaska. I'd better answer," he said, as he looked at the screen of his phone.

Immediately a swirl of unease went through her. Fear tightened the skin on her neck, and she was grateful for Travis's arm which was still around her.

"Hello?" Travis said, answering the phone and putting it on speaker so she could hear too.

"I have to go. You need to come back right now. I'll leave the children here. I have to leave."

"Relax. Is the house on fire?" Travis said, turning as he did so, like they needed to walk out of the pasture immediately.

"No."

"Are the kids in danger?" he asked, his words fast, staccato.

"No. Not right now. But they will be if I stay."

"Okay. Calm down. You don't have to leave before we get back. But we're coming right away. We'll be there in ten minutes."

"I can't wait ten minutes!"

She started to cry.

"You have to. There's no vehicle there for you anyway."

"I'll take Ellen's car. I need to go. I shouldn't have come to begin with. I just love my kids so much."

"If you need to call the police. Do it."

"He's not here now. But he said he was going to find me. He said he would know where I was, had heard about my children, and that he was coming for me."

Travis grabbed a hold of her hand and walked as fast as he could through the field toward where their car was parked. Ellen held on tight, and took a couple of jogging steps to keep up with him. She didn't want anything to happen to the children. She didn't know exactly what was going on with Alaska, but whatever it was, she didn't want that to touch the kids.

Wait. Was she saying what it sounded like she was saying?

"Is this little boy yours too?" Ellen asked, and Travis's eyes opened wide, as he glanced at her, never slowing his stride.

"Yes. I'm sorry. I know I really took advantage of you guys —"

"You didn't. We were happy to help. Now, if you're in danger, hang up right now and call the police. Otherwise, hold tight until we get there."

"I'll wait," Alaska said, quietly, almost whispered. "I'm scared."

"We'll be there. We're not going to let anything happen. Now, I'm going to go, because I'm going to call and get some help."

"Alright."

By that time they'd reached the truck. Travis opened her door, but didn't stay to close it for her. Rather, he ran around and jumped in on his side.

"If Tadgh is watching us, he's going to think we're rushing off to get married."

Travis laughed, although he had already started the truck and put it in reverse, backing up to get out.

On the seat, Chewy whined, lifting her head and looking at Ellen. It was like Chewy knew that there was a problem too.

"It's okay," she said, as much to calm herself as to calm Chewy.

"I'm going to call Ezra." Travis spoke as soon as he had it in forward gear, heading toward the highway.

Ellen wanted to ask why. She knew who Ezra was, and had met him a couple of times. His family, the Clyborne, consisted of twelve kids, including Ezra who was the oldest. From what Ellen understood, he was close to forty. She knew Travis had invested in their ranch, the Sweet View Ranch, and he and his siblings had been working hard to make it successful.

They had been supposed to move in eight years ago, but there had been some kind of hang up. She wasn't sure what it was. Maybe that was something she could talk to Travis about at some point, but she hadn't seen him long enough to run out of other things that she felt were more important. Like when they were going to get married.

"Hello?"

"Ezra. It's Travis." Travis's voice cut through her thoughts.

"Hey, man," Ezra said easily.

Ezra had always struck her as a quiet, confident man who was used to being in charge. As the oldest of twelve siblings, it stood to reason that he would need to have a commanding nature. Especially since from what Ellen understood, he had been the head of the family since their parents had been killed in a car accident.

"I have a woman who needs a job. She doesn't have any references, and... I can't even tell you for sure whether she's going to be a good worker. I just know that she's scared, and needs a safe place."

"Send her out to the ranch."

"I figured that's what you would say."

"It's gated, and with all the people and dogs around, we're not going to have someone come in without us knowing about it. If she has any kind of aptitude at all, I can put her to work as my personal assistant. I've been looking for one for a while. Just haven't taken the time to actually interview anyone."

"I can't vouch for how honest she is. Or anything."

"You send her out. We'll make sure that nothing happens to her. If she's not honest, I can't guarantee we'll give her a job, but at least she'll have food and a place to sleep."

"There's a hitch."

"Hit me."

"She might have two children with her." Travis's face squeezed like it pained him to say it, but Ellen agreed that the children should be with their mother if it was possible and she admired the sacrifice it obviously was for Travis to admit that. "One is a small baby."

There was silence on the line. Ellen found herself holding her breath. Was that going to ruin everything?

She almost opened her mouth and said that they could take care of the baby, even the little boy. They could take care of both of them. But, as a woman, she couldn't imagine walking away without her children and she didn't want to make Alaska do that.

"I'll make sure they're safe."

"Thank you."

"No problem. When you have details, you can let me know."

"I'll try to get what I can. I'll text you everything I know. Right now, I'm assuming it's the father of the children who is threatening her. But, she didn't actually say. I don't have a name."

"If you can get one, that'd be helpful. But, like I said, we'll keep her close, circle around her, and if someone wants to get her, they'll have to go through us first."

"I appreciate it."

They hung up, and Ellen watched the grass along the edge of the road speed by before she turned with questioning eyes.

"Ezra is a good man. I figured he'd help us out."

"It's too bad you couldn't give him more information."

"I'll give them what I can. But, that's a safe spot up there. It's far enough away that a person has to be deliberate about going there. And there's enough people on the ranch that someone will notice anything that's off. After all, everyone who works there is related, so if they see a stranger, it's going to stick out. Plus, they have a bunch of dogs. The barking is almost deafening when you pull in."

Ellen laughed. "You better not say too much about that. You might have a house like that."

"And I'll love every minute of it," he said, glancing across the seat at her, before he looked ahead, putting his turn signal on as his driveway rapidly approached.

"I've kind of fallen in love with that baby. The idea of her leaving with her hurts my heart, but I don't have any job for her. And now I'm planning a wedding."

Those words made warmth and happiness bubble up inside of Ellen, despite the fear and the tension that seemed to grip her throat and chest.

"I appreciate that consideration. But I admire you for taking responsibility, and doing something about it. Not thinking that it must be somebody else's problem."

"I guess that maybe the world might be a better place if we all try to take care of each other a little better, instead of looking the other way when someone needs help."

She nodded, loving that was his attitude. That it wasn't that he would just let someone else do it, so he wasn't interrupted, or inconvenienced in any way.

She didn't know how things were going to end, but she knew that Travis would do the right thing, no matter how hard that was. That, along with the deep trust that God was in control, gave her confidence and peace.

Chapter Twenty-Four

Travis pulled into his house far faster than he usually did. He'd come to care deeply for that baby, and the idea of anything happening to her had stirred every protective instinct he possessed. Not to mention, the panic in Alaska's voice had been concerning. It was obvious that she thought something very terrible could happen. Whoever she was dealing with most likely was someone who gave her a legitimate fear.

He'd seen some nasty things as he traveled the country and the world. It was shocking what humans were capable of doing to other humans. He did not understand it, didn't even want to try, other than to know that to see those things happen, was to know that the devil was indeed, loose and alive in the world. There was no way he could doubt it.

Thankfully, Ellen got out as quickly as he did, and they walked side-by-side up the rickety steps. The house was run down, most of the shutters had fallen off, there were weeds in the flowerbeds, the porch needed to be completely replaced, a person had to be careful where they stepped, that they didn't fall through any of the rotten boards. He'd seen mice in the house, although he had traps out for them, and he was pretty sure there was a spot in the roof that leaked. Several of the windows were cracked, and half the time the hot water heater barely got the water lukewarm.

There was just so much to fix, and he hadn't been in a big rush to fix it, because he was going to look for a farm to buy, discuss it with Ellen, and get married and move, eventually.

He wanted to do things right away, but he thought it would be more considerate to Ellen that way. But, she had thrilled him to the very bottom of his soul when she said that she preferred not to. Now, he had all kinds of things to do, and no time in which to do them.

But, if she would marry him and move into a house like this, then, he figured he'd let her.

"Alaska!" he called as he opened the door. She was the kind of woman who might have a pistol aimed at his head as he walked through. He didn't want her to mistake him for whoever she was so scared of.

He opened the door to silence.

Lord. Please don't let her have left with the children. Please keep them safe.

He prayed as he walked in, wondering belatedly if it was wise to have Ellen coming in with him. He didn't want anything to happen to her, after all the years they'd waited to be together. But not only that, he loved her. He couldn't stand the idea that she might get hurt.

But it was too late. Now, the safest place for her was probably right beside him. If he had to do it over again, he would've left her at her uncle's place, until he figured everything out. But he wasn't used to dealing with situations like this. He had been trained in business, not... Whatever this was.

"Travis?" a soft voice called from the living room. He didn't see any movement, as he started to walk slowly toward it, not wanting to push Ellen behind him, but tugging on her hand a little, to let her know that he would prefer she let him go first.

She glanced up at him as he tugged, and then she smiled, reassuringly. There was no fear at all in her eyes. He loved that. She might not be aware that there was danger, or she might just be confident that God was going to take care of them, no matter what happened. He preferred to think it was the second, just because he knew that was the kind of person Ellen was.

She moved without him tugging again and put two hands on either side of his waist as she followed him in.

He loved that she touched him, so he knew that she was still there and okay.

"Alaska?" he said as he reached the doorway of the living room.

She stood up from where she had been crouching behind the recliner.

"I'm so relieved," she said, on an exhale that showed how truly relieved she was.

"Everything's okay. I didn't see anything moving around in the yard as we came in." His eyes had swept the yard, but he hadn't searched diligently. He'd been thinking about the dilapidated house and bringing his bride home.

"The kids are sleeping." She pulled her bottom lip in, and gave him a glance, as Ellen came out from behind him and put her arm around his waist. He put his around her shoulders and pulled her tight against him. Still not wanting her to be any further from him than what she needed to be. Alaska was obviously scared.

"So sorry for bringing you guys into this. I shouldn't have come."

"No. You needed to come and get help. The police station would have been a good idea."

"If I go to the police station, the first thing he'll do is find my children and kill them."

"Who is he?"

She pulled both lips in and bit them.

"Chelmer Leggins."

Beside him he could feel Ellen stiffen at the name.

He didn't laugh, but he did let out a bit of a breath and almost snort. He would never have guessed that. Chelmer didn't seem like the kind of person to instill fear in people, but he did have a lot of bluster and brag. And, it didn't surprise Travis at all that he was probably wrapped up in drugs.

"Is he the father of your children?"

"Yeah."

She looked down. Like she was ashamed. He supposed it was

because she knew that Chelmer had children who are very much the same age as hers.

Which meant that she had been with him when he had been married to Shanna. What a mess.

"Has he threatened you?" Travis asked, trying to keep his words gentle and not strident.

"Yeah. Multiple times. He... Made me visit men, and..." Her voice trailed off.

"Basically he was your pimp," Travis said, and he suddenly felt very weary.

"Yeah."

"All right. That's enough. I don't know if he's capable of the things you seem to think he is, but I have a place where you will be safe. You can take your children if you want to, or you can leave them here with us."

"I'd...really like to take them. Where?" Alaska said.

"The Clyborne Ranch. It's called Sweet View, and I've spoken with Ezra. He's the head of the family, and he'll keep you with him. There are a bunch of people running around at the ranch. It's always busy, and there are plenty of dogs, plus the driveway is gated. People are not going to be getting in very easily. And I think you'll be safe there until we can figure out if we can get Chalmer out of the picture."

It made sense. If Chalmer had been making money as her pimp, and she left him, he lost an easy source of income. He didn't know how far Chalmer would go to try to get her back, but he doubted it was very far. The man wasn't known for his tenacity. But, it was probably better to be safe than sorry. Because Travis had seen men do crazy things, especially when there were drugs involved.

"I don't have any way of getting there," Alaska said, as though the thought had just occurred to her.

"I'll make sure you get there. It will probably take a couple of trips until we get the kids' stuff out, and get beds and things set up for them. Ezra is not married, doesn't have any children and I'm sure it's going to take a little time for him to be ready to have two kids."

"Alaska and I could take the kids and go look for a wedding dress.

We could go to Rockerton if you think you'd be safe there?" Ellen spoke up.

Travis thought that was a brilliant idea. He loved the idea of her getting a wedding dress herself, and he also thought it would be a good idea to get Alaska out somewhere where Chelmer wouldn't be looking for her.

"Bismark might be better."

"All right. Let's go to Bismark then. Will that work for you Travis?"

"Yeah. But leave the kids here. I'll call Ezra, we'll discuss it, and we'll get things ready so that when you come back, we'll have a spot for you at the Sweet View Ranch.

"How can I ever thank you?" Alaska said.

"Well, I originally told Ezra that you were looking for a job. He was willing to give you one as his personal assistant. You'd probably be in charge of keeping all the books for the ranch, and possibly cooking meals, I don't know. This seems like it could be a new start for you. Something you might be interested in. It would be a good place for you to raise your children, and Ezra is an honest and upright man. So, the way you could repay me is by doing a good job. Being honest, and trustworthy. I couldn't tell him you are, because I don't know you. So he'll be watching. I know he'll give you the benefit of the doubt, but he probably won't give that to you twice."

Alaska nodded her head, and Travis hoped he hadn't been too hard on her. He was trying to emphasize the fact that if she wanted to turn her life around, she was the one who had to do it. She couldn't sit around waiting for someone else to fix her. She had to take the initiative.

Of course, it was easier for a Christian to do that, because they had the Holy Spirit helping them. Still, Alaska would be in an environment where she would surely hear about Jesus, if she hadn't already, and she could make a decision for herself.

As much as Travis wanted to discuss it with her now, God gave a person free choice, and that's what he needed to do as well. Wait on God's timing.

"Do you need to get ready to go?" His voice softened as he looked at Ellen. She glowed, her cheeks were rosy, her eyes shone, and she looked at him with so much...love in her eyes that it made his heart feel like it was too big for his chest, and all he wanted to do was pull her close and never let her go.

"No. I'm ready now."

"All right. The two of you can go, and I'll call the police, let them know what's going on. They might want to talk to you when you get back. I don't know...I've never handled anything like this before. But after that, I'll call Ezra and we'll go from there."

Chapter Twenty-Five

"You should try that one on," Ellen said.

Alaska looked where her fingers touched the satin material. Her fingers did not seem to go with the silk and elegance of the wedding gown.

"No. I couldn't. I'm not getting married anytime soon."

"It doesn't matter. It's fun to try fancy dresses on. And if I'm going to try one on, you can too."

Alaska looked at the bridal attendant. "Go ahead. You never know when you'll fall in love with a dress and want to sock it away for your own wedding."

"Until I get married, I probably wouldn't fit in this dress anyway."

"Tell me your size. If you buy the dress we'll make sure it fits you, but at the very least, you can feel like a princess for a few minutes."

The wedding attendant was sweet, and since they were the only ones in the shop, they were getting all of her attention.

Ellen seemed a little uncomfortable with it, and Alaska assumed that was just the way she was. She didn't seem like the kind of girl who would want a big fancy gown, but Alaska had to admit she'd been having fun. She almost felt like a kid again.

Although her childhood was so far away, and her innocence so long-lost, that it was hard to remember exactly what being a child felt like.

A little bit of bitterness welled up in her throat. Bitterness at the things that she had been forced to do. Bitterness at how her life turned out. A lot of the mistakes that she'd made she had no one to blame but herself, but she had started down this road because of her home life.

She pushed that aside, and tried to focus on the innocent fun of the day. Her children were in good hands, and she was actually doing something that she never thought she would. Trying on wedding dresses.

The dresses were complicated and difficult, and it was thirty minutes before the two of them were out of the changing areas and looking at each other across the wide room with all the mirrors.

She could see herself, front and back, as the angles of the mirror were situated for that type of view. The gown contained rows of lace and pearls and sequins and was much more frilly and feminine than anything she would pick out. The bottom of it puffed out, like every little girl's dream, and she truly did feel like a princess. She couldn't imagine wearing something like this every day, but she believed she could get used to it.

"You look gorgeous in that. Like you were born to wear it," Ellen said, meeting Alaska's eyes in the mirror.

"I feel like a princess," Alaska said, even though the sleeves of her tattoos clashed with the gown. It was sleeveless, and while she had loved her tattoos when she got them, they didn't really represent who she was now. They definitely didn't look right with the dress.

"You look perfect in yours," she said, and she hoped what she felt didn't come out in her voice too much.

It was true though. Ellen with her pristine skin, looked like she was born to wear the white dress she had on. She looked as innocent as the dress proclaimed her to be.

It made Alaska jealous. Not jealous in that she wanted to hurt Ellen, because Ellen had been nothing but kind to her, but jealous in a way that she wished that she would have had Ellen's life. If she would have had a start like Ellen's, she could look like that, too. Instead, she looked exactly like she was, someone who had lived a lot of life, and lived it in places where there wasn't a lot of love and kindness to go around.

She wanted better for her children. Hopefully, this opportunity that Travis had opened for her would give her the ability to offer a better life for her children. Maybe someday one of them would go into a bridal shop somewhere, try on a gown, and look like they were born to wear it.

She could only hope that was in Alice's future. She wanted Alice to be like Ellen, not like herself.

"I don't know. It just feels... Too much."

"It looks perfect on you. And we wouldn't even really need to do too many alterations. Maybe a little tuck here, and possibly letting the hem out just an inch or so, depending on how high your heels are."

"I haven't decided about that," Ellen said, a little shyly.

"We have a great selection, and I can bring you some samples."

"I think maybe I'll think about it. I really appreciate all the time you've put into us."

The sales lady smiled benevolently, and continued to adjust the long train of Ellen's dress.

"What do you think?" Ellen asked as she looked over at Alaska.

"I agree. I think maybe I've had enough for now, and we need to think about it."

"I'm starving. Maybe we can have lunch and make a decision while we eat."

"Food always makes decisions easier," the sales lady said as she stood back and admired the picture Ellen made as she stood with her dress perfectly arranged. "But I can say this is most definitely the nicest gown that you've tried on."

"It's also the most expensive," Ellen said, with a self-conscious laugh.

"That's true. Quality isn't cheap," the sales lady said, and to Alaska it sounded like a rehearsed comment.

It was another forty-five minutes before they had the gowns off and their regular clothing back on and they walked out of the store.

"You could afford to buy any gown in there," Alaska said. She didn't know exactly how much money Travis had, but the rumor around town was that he was a multimillionaire. Perhaps a billionaire, and there was no doubt in anyone's mind that Ford Hansen was a billionaire. Travis was practically his son. Everyone knew it.

"I don't know about that. I suppose Travis could. And I guess he'd probably buy it for me if I wanted him to. But... I don't know. That just seems like such a lot of money to spend on a dress I'm only going to wear once. And, I don't really care about the dress."

"You don't want to look beautiful?"

"Oh. That's not true. I love looking like a princess. Feeling like a princess. But...there just seems to be so many other more worthy things to spend money on. I just don't want to waste it on a dress. Not that kind of money." Ellen hooked her arm in Alaska's, and they walked down the street together.

"What kind of food are you hungry for?" Ellen asked as they strolled casually, looking in the store windows at the displays of dresses and business suits and nursing uniforms, passing other shoppers who carried armfuls of packages, and chatted excitedly with the friends they strolled with.

Alaska couldn't remember if she ever walked on the street and had nothing more to do than just look at the windows and have not a care in the world.

"I'm so hungry I really don't care. Anything sounds good to me."

"I think there's a Chinese place up ahead. Will that work?" Ellen asked.

"Sure."

"I guess I do have to wear a dress. I'm just not sure —" Ellen cut off in mid sentence.

Alaska looked at her, and saw that her gaze was caught by something across the street.

Alaska followed her gaze over and saw that she was looking in the window of a second hand store, where a wedding dress was prominently displayed on a mannequin in the window.

"That one is pretty," Ellen said. She nodded across the street. "Do you see it?"

"I do. Do you want a used wedding dress?"

"Sure. Why not?" Ellen said, tugging on Alaska's arm as they went to the crosswalk and crossed to the other side.

"I don't know. It's... A wedding dress. Isn't it supposed to be just yours?"

"I don't think so. Is there some kind of etiquette law that I don't know about?"

"Well, just... Someone else might have said vows in that dress."

"And so it's broken in. It knows what to do. Just in case I faint, the dress can handle the rest of the ceremony for me."

They laughed together and Alaska had to bite her tongue. Ellen could afford any dress she wanted, and she was going to seriously consider one in the window of the second hand store?

Not only did she seriously consider it, but after they went in and tried it on, Ellen purchased it. She paid less than a hundred dollars for it, when the ones that they had been looking at in the bridal shop were in the five figures.

The store clerk didn't even have a proper bag to package it in, so she ended up putting a garbage bag over the top of it and poking the hanger through, and then folding up the bottom of the dress and putting it in another garbage bag and tying the two together.

"You have your wedding dress in a garbage bag," Alaska said as they walked out of the store. She had to admit, she thought that Ellen was a little bit...too good for her. Too classy. But, seeing what Ellen had just done had made her much more relatable.

"I do. And, this makes me so much happier."

"A cheap, used, wedding dress and a garbage bag makes you happier than the brand-new beautiful dresses that we tried on earlier?" She wasn't sure she understood that.

"Yeah. This doesn't offend my... I don't even know. But it just makes me happy to think that I have a pretty dress that didn't cost more than some people's cars."

"Well, I have to keep that in mind, if I ever seriously need a dress of my own."

"Well, you know I've got one if you need it, and I'm not overly attached to it, so if you want it, it's yours."

They had been about the same size, although she was a little taller and slightly broader in the shoulders than Ellen.

Still, Alaska felt like she was having a girls day out with someone who was not out of her league after all.

This was the kind of wedding dress that she could have afforded. Although having a wedding dress was not something that she ever really thought about. Chalmer had promised her that he was divorcing Shanna and would marry her, but of course that was a lie, just like everything else that he ever promised her.

It was almost too good to be true that she could be away from him for good and safe as well.

She never met this Ezra person that Travis talked about, but Travis had seemed so confident in his ability to take care of her that Alaska hadn't even questioned it. At the very least, she could get herself and her children there, get back on their feet, and maybe move to a different state. Somewhere where they would leave Chalmer and those problems behind. Somewhere where she wouldn't be recognized for the things that she had done.

She wouldn't want her children to suffer because of the choices that she'd made. Even if she felt like she had no choice at the time.

Of course, some of the things that she'd done were a lot more socially acceptable than they used to be. Maybe her children would suffer more because she decided to turn her back on all those things and go down a different path...choosing Jesus. She almost laughed at the irony.

Regardless, she tried to pull her mind away from those things, and enjoy her lunch with Ellen. She almost felt like she and Ellen really could be friends.

Chapter Twenty-Six

"I already called the police. She's not going to like it, but when they get home from shopping, we're going to take a trip into the station." Travis hadn't wanted to do it, but Sweet Water didn't have their own police force so they'd have to go to Rockerton.

Still, he talked to Ford, and they agreed that there should be a record of the issues. Not to mention, they didn't want to send her to the Sweet View Ranch if she were hiding something dangerous. Something beyond just Chalmer.

"All right. If you need me to come pick her up, I can."

"I should be able to drop her off." Travis had a million things to do, but Ezra was doing them a favor, and he didn't want to put the man out any more than what they had to.

He looked around the room. Ezra had a small home of his own behind the larger farmhouse. They had agreed that it would be safer for Alaska, at least at first, to stay there. Officially she was going on the books as his housekeeper. But, considering that he was just one man, and the farmhouse wasn't massive, there wasn't much housekeeping to be done. He would probably end up giving her other things to do, but Travis didn't really care. He knew Ezra would be fair, and Alaska would be treated well there.

"You know, if you and Ellen are getting married as quickly as what you said, why don't you do it here?" Ezra shoved his hands in his pockets and leaned his shoulder against the door jamb that led from the dining room into the kitchen.

"That's fine with me. As long as it's okay with Ellen. Are you sure? You guys are already busy."

"Well, I've been kind of wondering what in the world I'm going to get this woman to do. I mean, as a housekeeper to me, you see the house. It's not that big. And one man doesn't need that much. Planning a wedding might give her something to do, and it would make her feel a little bit more like she's a part of the ranch right off. But it would also keep her behind the scenes."

"I see." He appreciated that Ezra had thought it through.

Having Alaska stay with Ezra wasn't ideal in his opinion. But Ezra was almost forty, and while he didn't know Alaska's exact age, he would guess her to be in her mid-twenties. The fifteen years between them probably was a good buffer. Not that he thought that Ezra would do anything untoward. Alaska he wasn't sure about.

"All right. Talk to Ellen, see what she thinks. Give me a call, and make sure I'm here before you come with Alaska. If you think about it."

"I'll do it." They shook hands, and then Travis walked out. He had some other things he needed to talk to Ezra about. Business things about the ranch, but those things could wait for another day.

Ellen texted him as he put the baby in his truck to say she was on her way.

He was tempted to tell her to meet him at the police station in Rockerton, but he figured that it would be best for him to take them. He buckled Eugene in, while the child chattered and he responded as needed.

Doing everything with two small children made life a lot more difficult, but he had to admit that he was looking forward to Ellen and him having children. He was looking forward to that family thing. Of doing it with Ellen. He definitely wouldn't be looking forward to it with anyone else.

He couldn't imagine that.

Before he pulled out, he sent her a text.

Did you get a dress?

Yes.

He smiled as he pulled out on the road. He couldn't wait to see Ellen in her wedding dress. Standing and waiting for him. There might be a small part of him that was nervous, that, like he told Ellen, was concerned about the responsibility. After all, marriage was a covenant instituted by God, and he would be answering to God for the way he handled his role as husband and father. If that didn't scare a man, he didn't know what would. But, he appreciated what Ellen was giving to him. She was voluntarily linking her life with his, and agreeing to submit to his authority.

It was a big step for both of them, and definitely not something he would want to enter into lightly, or with someone who didn't have the character that Ellen did. It didn't feel like they were rushing, considering that Ellen had been the one that he had wanted for the last eight years.

He got home well before she did, and, as he figured, Alaska did not want to go to the police station, but she agreed for him to drive her. Ellen stayed at the house watching the children, although he kind of wanted her to go along. There was a little bit of unease about leaving her there. While he didn't believe that the threats Alaska had received from Chalmer were serious, he didn't want to dismiss the fact that the man could be dangerous.

It didn't take long for the police to get all the information they could from Alaska. Travis was not an expert, but he felt like Alaska was being as truthful as possible. He also felt that she wanted to put that behind her.

The ride home was quiet, as he tried to figure out whether he should try to talk to her or not.

"I know that Ellen would agree with me, that if things don't work out at Sweet View Ranch, you're always welcome to come back and stay with us. I don't want you to feel like you don't have any other options." He knew when someone felt like their back was against the wall they might do things that they would regret. Brash things that weren't the smartest decisions.

"You guys have already done so much for me. I could hardly impose more."

"It wouldn't be imposing. I know I can speak for Ellen too. We both like you, we love your children, and we want to see you be successful. We'll do what we can to help you." He supposed he could just give her a big wad of money, but when a person got money without working for it, they just didn't seem to have the character to know how to use it. That's what he'd seen, over and over again. In his opinion it was one of the reasons government programs didn't work.

"I wish you guys would stop being so nice. While I appreciate it, it just makes me feel like I'm going to owe you more than I could ever repay. I don't like to be in debt."

"No one is expecting you to repay anything. Just pass it on when you can. Plus, you can just consider that we're doing it for your children if that makes you feel better."

"You know, today, Ellen tried on some really beautiful gowns. Beautiful and expensive gowns. It shocked me when she chose not to go with any of those, but instead bought a gown for less than a hundred bucks at a secondhand store. Before that, I felt like you and Ellen were... Out of my league. Too high and mighty for me. Watching her do that, and she didn't do it for show, or because she thought she was going to impress me. She did it because that's the unpretentious kind of person she is. I... I felt like I could relate to someone like that. You know? Like, even though I wanted to be like that, where, I am less concerned about the things I have, and more thoughtful about how I can help people. That's just what she impressed me with over and over today."

"That's Ellen." He smiled, thinking about what a wonderful person Ellen was. And how blessed he was that he was going to get to call her his wife.

She had supper on the stove when they walked in, and they talked for a while around the table, with Alaska and him telling her what happened at the police station, and her and Alaska telling him about their shopping trip.

It was late when they dropped Alaska and the kids off at the Sweet View Farm, and he knew that he would have to take Ellen and drop her off at her house. He didn't want to spend even another minute without her, but hopefully soon dropping her off would be a thing of the past.

There were a lot of things they needed to talk about, but for now, he was content to hold her hand in the darkness of the pickup, and just ride in silence, enjoying the fact that they were together. And that their life stretched out ahead of them, filled with hope and possibilities and a beautiful, sacrificial love that most people only dreamed about.

Chapter Twenty-Seven

"I now pronounce you man and wife. You may kiss your bride."

Travis leaned down as Ellen lifted her head, and the crowd cheered as they kissed.

Alaska had spent a whirlwind three days trying to coordinate everything that had led to this moment.

She'd been kind of dropped in the middle of everything, with two small children to boot, but she remembered what Travis had said about Ezra taking a chance on her, and she didn't want to let the man down.

Actually, in the three days that she'd been there, she'd barely seen him, but when she had... She wanted to sigh every time. He was the kind of man a girl could have daydreams about.

Except, he would not look at her and think of her as anything other than someone that he needed to help. He would never consider her as any type of romantic interest.

A man like Ezra did not marry a girl like her. Particularly since she already had two children to someone else. Someone else's *husband*.

That was the kind of thing that Ezra would never consider doing. Not in a million years. She'd been around him enough to know that he was as moral and upright as a person could be. She laughed a little, since he reminded her somewhat of Abraham Lincoln. Or maybe that other general in the war. What was his name? Grant, she thought.

Wasn't he a president too?

She couldn't remember, but it didn't matter. He just reminded her of someone who was old-fashioned, upright, very moral, and very strict.

She admired him, for sure. He ran the ranch with an iron hand. There were a lot of things that needed help, improvements that had to be made, and he was busy from the time she got up in the morning until she left his house at night. She didn't know what time he got up, or what time he went to bed. She never saw him except when he was working.

Part of her wanted to see if she could get him to take a break once in a while. It would be healthier for him. Maybe that's what she should do. She'd been wondering what in the world she was going to do to keep herself busy once the wedding was over. Maybe, taking on Ezra and his health would be a good start.

Who was she kidding? That was just an excuse to get to work with him even closer than what she had been. Or maybe she just wanted to see him interact with her children more. As taciturn and serious as he was, it was adorable to see him with the kids. There was a gentle, soft side of him that came out when he interacted with the baby, Alice, and it melted her heart every single time.

Travis and Ellen pulled back and smiled into each other's eyes, before the preacher announced, "May I present, Mr. and Mrs. Travis Feagley."

The crowd cheered again.

She called it a crowd, but it was basically the Clyborne family, as well as people from Sweet Water. Anyone who could get off at such short notice. They put everything together in three days, which had been quite a feat, and while she certainly hadn't done all the work herself, she felt like she'd made it possible.

"You did a good job," a voice said beside her, while a heavy hand landed on her shoulder.

Alice slept in the car seat by her feet, while Eugene held her other hand and she tried not to startle as she turned and looked up into the dark eyes of Ezra. Even though she knew he must be almost forty, and was way too old for her, even if he would have been interested in a woman like her, since she was just twenty-six, her heart still raced.

"Thank you," she said, knowing that she sounded breathless, but trying to cover it. Telling herself it was because he startled her, and not because that was what happened to her whenever he was around.

"You deserve a day off. You've crammed two weeks of work into three days. You do that, and then come to my office the day after tomorrow, and we'll talk about your future."

She nodded, blinking, and trying to process what he said, and she didn't get any words out before he walked away.

Was he going to send her off somewhere else? That's kind of what it sounded like.

She'd been a little nervous about today, but Ezra had assured her that the guests were being checked, and that they would specifically be looking for Chalmer.

He hadn't said they would keep Chalmer out, but she felt safe nonetheless.

Her heart continued to beat erratically, as her eyes refused to leave the man, watching as he walked away. Tall, straight, wearing blue jeans and a button-down, his head covered with a cowboy hat, and his feet in worn boots.

It really wasn't the way he wore them, it was the confident way he walked. The quiet way that he retained authority without resorting to a lot of yelling, or even a lot of words. He barely ever said more than three or four sentences at one time, and she hadn't heard any profanity out of him, or anyone else on the ranch, at all.

It was an entirely new world for her. One she was determined to fit in.

As long as she could keep from falling in love with her boss.

Join Jessie's list and be the first to know about new releases and sales on her books!

Read *A Cowboy's Growing Grace*, the next book in the Sweet View Ranch series featuring Ezra, a man of principles and routine, and Alaska, whose big troubles are about to turn his world upside down. Will love thrive amidst threats faced together?

Sneak Peek of A Cowboy's Growing Grace

"Ezra, you remember Terry Clomp? The girl that has the cubicle across from me?" Sondra didn't wait for his answer, which was just fine by Ezra. He had no clue who Terry was. "She told me that she and her boyfriend are finally moving in together. They've been dating for six months, and she's been staying at his place most nights. And paying for her own apartment."

She paused, and he assumed this was where he was supposed to interject some kind of sound into the conversation.

"Hmm."

"I hope it doesn't interrupt our weekly Tuesday night dinners. That's when we catch up on all the latest and watch the best series in the world, and you know what that is."

He had no idea.

"Hmm."

"Exactly. *The Bedroom and Beyond.* The actors of that show are just amazing, and the writers are perfect. Especially Bubba Goo, the most gorgeous man in the world." She sighed. Ezra supposed it was a dreamy sigh. "He's absolutely perfect, and I would just die to spend one second with him."

Sondra went on, and Ezra tried to pay attention. It was hard, because he had no clue what she was talking about. He didn't even own a TV, let alone watch one. And it seemed like every couple of weeks, Sondra's best friend changed, and he couldn't keep up.

"So," the tone of her voice shifted, and he tried to pay attention. "When are you going to invite me out? I thought you said that it was going to take you a little while to get settled in and then you were going to have me come out for a visit. I assume," her voice took on a teasing yet questioning quality, "that is so that I can look around and figure out where we'll live when we get married."

He cleared his throat. He liked Sondra, but as he looked around his office, it was primitive, and very cold in the winter, as was the rest of the house. And the entire farm actually. Considering that it was in North Dakota, everything was cold in the winter. But they were just coming out of the long, cold snowy season, and he really didn't have an excuse.

He liked her, but the idea of having her on the farm for a couple of days, or more, made him want to turn and run in the opposite direction. He would have to entertain her, lead her around, be by her side every waking second, and he didn't have time for that.

"Well, I want to make sure that things are ready for you," he hedged. There was something wrong with him. It wasn't Sondra. All of his siblings teased him that he was never going to get married. Maybe that was the reason that he'd not shut her down the first time she tried to talk to him. Or maybe it was because he knew they would be moving soon and didn't think they would stay together.

Whichever it was, he felt like a heel. Probably because he was one. He should just tell her now that he didn't want her to come out and that maybe they should start seeing other people. And she'd blindsided him when she assumed they were going to get married. Except, she was already talking again by the time he got his mouth open

"That's so sweet of you. That's one of the things I love about you. You're so protective, just like the hero in my favorite movie." And then she went off on a tangent describing her favorite movie.

He started to sigh and managed to stop himself just in time, before he did it into the mouthpiece of his phone.

She was still describing the first act, as far as he could tell, when his brother Asher walked into his office.

He held up one finger, indicating to Asher that he would be with him in a moment.

He waited for Sondra to take a breath.

"I'm sorry. I need to go."

"Aww," she pouted. "All right. I'll text you later and let you know how the tournament turns out. And I'll send you pictures of the shoes that I bought. You can let me know which ones are your favorites. I'll be sure to pack them when we nail down a date."

"All right," he said.

They hung up, and Ezra stared at his phone for just a moment. He really needed to tell Sondra that they just weren't going to work out.

"She trying to come out again?" Asher asked with a perception that irritated Ezra. He was really good at seeing things that needed to be done, figuring out the best ways to do things, and working his butt off.

People, women in particular, seemed to be beyond his ability to figure out.

A person would have thought, considering that he was the oldest of twelve children, and that he had six sisters, including two twin sisters who were barely two years younger than him, he would have a little bit of something figured out.

But his brain just didn't seem to work the way that it needed to in order to understand the gentler sex.

Actually, he didn't find females to be all that much more gentle than males.

But his grunt seemed to be answer enough, because Asher grinned, picking up the stapler that was on Ezra's desk and straightening it up before he set it back down. "You know, if you're going to get married to her, you probably ought to look forward to seeing her and try to figure out how you can be together, not to mention, you should enjoy her company."

Right. He probably knew that. But he was content to call her his girlfriend, talk to her once in a while, or maybe just a little bit more often, and live in one state while she lived four states away.

Yeah, that probably wasn't the best foundation for a marriage.

"You don't usually have trouble getting things done," Asher commented, lifting his brows and looking down his nose at Ezra.

The look made Ezra push away from his desk and stand to his feet. Asher was eight years younger than he was and a half an inch shorter. With a conversation like this, Ezra felt like he needed every inch of his height.

"And I'll get that done too. You're right."

"Yeah. If you can get a word in edgewise. Never met anyone who could talk as much as Sondra can." Asher lifted one brow. "Even Joanna," he said, referring to their second youngest sister. Joanna was number eleven of twelve, and Ezra figured that she probably had to do a lot of talking in order to get noticed

But Asher was correct. Even Joanna couldn't outtalk Sondra.

Or maybe it was just that Joanna said things Ezra was interested in or could get interested in. The latest TV show or the perfect style of shoe was not something that would help him run his ranch and therefore was not something about which he had much to say.

"Excuse me." The door pushed open. Alaska, whom he had just hired to be his personal assistant, popped her head in the door.

"Come on in," Ezra said, figuring that whatever Asher had to say could wait.

"I just wasn't sure whether you wanted me to file those folders in alphabetical order or by date," she said, one hand reaching out to twirl the earring in her lobe.

She had piercings in her upper ears as well, but she didn't seem to mess with those. That was something he'd noticed in the last four days she'd been there.

"File the ones with the names on them in alphabetical order. File the ones that have general information by date," he said, remembering that she was working on the bulls he'd used in his herd for the last four years, as well as the different updates that they'd done to the ranch so far, since they had bought it almost a year prior.

They had been going to buy it almost eight years before, but things had gotten held up when they tried to sell their farm in Wyoming.

If they hadn't, he probably wouldn't have gotten entangled with Sondra.

He tried to push that thought out of his head. He wasn't through with Sondra, and maybe things would work out after all. Since all the problems were on his end, he was responsible for trying to fix them.

He knew there were defects in his personality, and if Sondra was willing to put up with him, he should put more of an effort into their relationship. So far, she hadn't complained, but he could see a lot of room for improvement.

"Ezra?" Alaska's voice came again.

"Yes?" he said, noting that she was playing with her earring again.

"You told me to tell you when the kids were sleeping because you wanted to go over what my duties were going to be. They're sleeping."

He kept himself from smiling. For some reason, he had been looking forward to talking with her. They had hosted a wedding on short notice on the ranch, and she had spearheaded everything. He'd been impressed by her organizational skills and her ability to jump in and do whatever needed to be done, while rolling with the things that didn't work out. She didn't get upset, and while she was understandably hassled, it wasn't in a grumpy or short-tempered way. He admired her.

She obviously made some interesting choices in her life, but a person could argue that so had he.

"Let me finish talking to my brother, and I'll come find you."

The door closed behind her, and Ezra noticed for the first time that Asher had a smirk on his face.

"What's so funny?" he asked, making sure he was standing to his full height as he crossed his arms over his chest.

"Are you really hiring her?" Asher said, rather than answer his question.

"I said I would. She needs a place to stay where she'll be protected."

"You realize that whoever's after her is probably some kind of drug dealer?"

"That's kind of judgmental, don't you think?"

"Sometimes judgmental is accurate. I'm not maligning her character, I'm just asking. After all, my family lives and works here. And I have a vested interest in keeping them safe. I thought you did too."

The smirk had vanished from Asher's face, and his expression was serious.

None of them ever took the safety of their family for granted, and for the Clybourns, family had always come first. Even ahead of helping people, although they'd never shirk from doing that either.

"You're right," he acknowledged, knowing that sometimes a person earned a reputation, and they looked it. "But she has two small children and nowhere to go. Someone was threatening her, just threats. I said she would be safe here, and I believe she will be."

"But will we?"

"Do you want me to tell her to go?"

"I just don't trust the way you were looking at her."

"What do you mean?" Ezra's eyes narrowed. He really had no idea what his brother was saying.

"You were looking at her the way you should be looking at Sondra, except you look bored out of your mind when you're on the phone with Sondra. I don't even have to hear any of the conversation. I just look at your face, and I know it's her."

Ezra took two steps and turned toward the window, looking out on the green fields of the ranch where horses grazed in the distance, separated from a field of cattle by a section of fence. They worked long and hard to get that fence up. And they had a lot more to put in. But the ranch was looking a lot better than it had been when they moved in. Which was the idea. Ford Hansen along with Travis Baker had invested in them, and he didn't want to let them down.

"I was concerned that you have her here because you feel something for her. And not because you're trying to keep her safe. And sometimes that means that you forget what your actual responsibilities are."

"You're talking like that's happened before. We both know it hasn't."

"Just because it hasn't happened before doesn't mean there won't be a first time."

Ezra jerked his head, without turning around to look at his brother. Those words were true. It was an arrogant man who thought that something could never happen to him. Ezra had been around long enough to know that about the time he thought he was immune to something, he would come down with it.

"What do you suggest I do?" he asked, without turning around. He wanted to be humble enough to ask his younger brother for advice and to take it seriously. In his mind, part of being a good leader was humility.

Sign up for Jessie's newsletter! Get a free book, access to exclusive bonus content, get fun and funny updates on her life on the farm and more!

A Gift from Jessie

View this code through your smart phone camera to be taken to a page where you can download a FREE ebook when you sign up to get updates from Jessie Gussman! Find out why people say, "Jessie's is the only newsletter I open and read" and "You make my day brighter. Love, love, love reading your newsletters. I don't know where you find time to write books. You are so busy living life. A true blessing." and "I know from now on that I can't be drinking my morning coffee while reading your newsletter – I laughed so hard I sprayed it out all over the table!"

Claim your free book from Jessie!